SWEET DESTINY

THIEF OF HEARTS BOOK 4

C.R. JANE

MILA YOUNG

Sweet Destiny by C. R. Jane and Mila Young

Copyright © 2021 by C. R. Jane and Mila Young

All rights reserved.

Cover art created by Covers by Aura

Edited by Briann Graziano

Visit our books at
www.milayoungbooks.com

www.crjanebooks.com

CONTENTS

Join Our Readers' Group — ix
Thief of Hearts — xi
Sweet Destiny — xiii

Chapter 1 — 1
Chapter 2 — 13
Chapter 3 — 24
Chapter 4 — 31
Chapter 5 — 44
Chapter 6 — 54
Chapter 7 — 64
Chapter 8 — 75
Chapter 9 — 83
Chapter 10 — 102
Chapter 11 — 118
Chapter 12 — 142
Chapter 13 — 151
Chapter 14 — 160
Chapter 15 — 171
Epilogue — 188

Wild Moon — 197
Acknowledgments — 199
C.R. Jane — 201
Mila Young — 203

DEDICATION

*For our readers who saw the cages they'd created for themselves
and decided to set themselves free.*

JOIN OUR READERS' GROUP

Stay up to date with C.R. Jane by joining her Facebook readers' group, C.R.'s Fated Realm. Ask questions, get first looks at new books/series, and have fun with other book lovers!

www.facebook.com/groups/C.R.FatedRealm

Join Mila Young's Wicked Readers Group to chat directly with Mila and other readers about her books, enter giveaways, and generally just have loads of fun!

www.facebook.com/groups/milayoungwickedreaders

THIEF OF HEARTS

Sweet Destiny
Stolen Destiny
Broken Destiny
Sweet Destiny

SWEET DESTINY

One man broke me. One led me to sin. And one killed me to save me.

I grew up under the thumb of a vampire. And when I betrayed him, I ended up in Nightmare Penitentiary.

Multiple attacks, my death, and four psycho men later, and I've had enough of being everyone's target.

I have to escape the monsters who surround me within these walls. So I took a chance... a deadly one in order to find my freedom.

My time to run has come to an end. With my fae prince, incubus, hellhound, and serial killer, I'm set to unleash hell on everyone who's stood against me.

Sometimes all you need is a second chance to make things right. But in my case, I was given four...

CHAPTER 1

SELENA

The sky seemed to darken the closer we got to the Chicago skyline. I'd always hated this city, hated everything about it. And my feelings hadn't changed while in prison.

The breeze coming off Lake Michigan pushed hair into my face. The car we were in traveled the road that ran right by the shore. I sighed enviously as I watched the families frolicking in the sand. I couldn't fathom that level of carefreeness. And the sight of the water just did something to me. Water always had that effect on me.

The car all of a sudden turned off the main road and headed towards a parking lot right by the water.

"What are we doing?" I asked Keon in surprise. I half expected to burst into flames from whatever spell the Warden had put on me to make sure I didn't get away.

The Warden didn't realize that I'd left a few pieces of myself behind at the prison. I missed Seth and Alaric... and Laz. I still was having trouble admitting that one to myself.

"We have some time before the funeral. And I know how you like the water."

My heart did a funny pitter-patter in my chest as I stared at Keon in amazement. "Is this allowed?" I asked, a little bit of sarcasm leaking into my voice.

He pulled the car into a parking spot and put the car into park. He stared at the water for a long moment, so long I thought that he wasn't going to answer my question.

"Just say the word, and we'll get out of here," he finally said. "We'll run as far away as we can, and we won't look back." His voice took on a pleading tone. "I'll find a way to remove the tracker. And we'll be free." Keon took my hand and pulled me towards him. "Say the word, Selena. And we'll do it."

For a second, I let myself imagine what it would be like, Keon and I on the run. I imagined always looking over our shoulders, a life in crummy motels where we had to pay in cash, a life where we always expected someone to crash through the front door.

The Warden would get tired of looking for us at some point, right?

Alaric's face appeared in my mind. Then Seth's. Then Laz's. Every moment I'd experienced with them ran like a movie through my mind.

"I can't," I finally whispered, a bit of heartbreak leaking in my voice. I felt like the biggest idiot on the planet. I wasn't just the girl who'd fallen for the bad boy. I was the girl who'd fallen for four of the worst kinds of bad boys, and who was literally willing to throw away a chance at freedom to stay with them. What was wrong with me?

Some of my mother's words chose that moment to

rear their ugly heads. "The day you give your heart away is the day you become the biggest kind of fool." She'd said it once when she'd come back from a visit with a client who liked to rough up his girls during sex. Apparently, he got off on his lover's tears and screams. My mother had a haunted look on her face when she'd come into my room that night, a giant black eye that had taken forever to heal on her face. I'd come home from school, excited for some reason to tell her about a new boy that had shown up, and how he'd said I was pretty. She'd snapped at me when I'd told her and then gave me those words. I guess it made sense that I would think about that now.

She'd be so disappointed if she could see me right now.

"Selena, baby," Keon whispered, and I realized that I had tears streaming down my face.

"I don't know why I'm crying. She was a terrible woman who seemed to thrive on my misery," I told him haltingly. "I think it's because I still must have been holding out some hope that someday she would change. That someday, maybe, she would have loved me. And now that's not possible." A hiccupped sob burst out of me. "It's so stupid that I would still feel that way."

"My dad killed my mother," Keon told me, and my gaze flicked up to his face, shocked. "And when he was sentenced to death, I was still upset about it, even though he was a monster. Even though he beat my mother and me every day of our lives. It's just ingrained in us as living beings, this desire to be loved by our parents. We're taught from birth that they're supposed to love us more than anything. So, when they don't, it twists something inside of us, creates a chasm that's impossible to feel. It's not stupid to miss the promise of someone, Selena. Even if that promise was probably not going to ever come true."

A wave of affection rushed over me. It was nice when someone gave you permission to feel. That didn't happen very often.

"I love you," I said softly, the words tasting strange on my tongue.

Keon's entire being lit up like a freaking Christmas tree. "I love you too, Selena. Always."

We stared at each other, probably looking like a pair of lovesick fools to anyone passing by our car. But I didn't care.

"If there weren't people everywhere I'd strip you naked and fuck the living daylight out of you," Keon suddenly swore. A snort slipped past my lips.

Ever the romantic my guy was.

"Let's go for a walk in the sand. We're running out of time," Keon said, a smile on his lips.

I nodded and walked out, still in shock at how amazing the sun felt on my skin. I took off my heels and threw them on the seat, desperate to feel the sand and the water on my skin. A giggle burst out of my throat as I ran towards the water's edge, practically shrieking in joy as a wave brushed across my legs. The bottom of my black dress got soaked, but I didn't care. Even a siren without her magic could feel the power in the waves. Humans experienced a small piece of it. Doctors in the old days had been onto something when they'd sent their sick patients to stay by the ocean for long periods of time. The water really had been healing them.

If only it could heal a heart.

"Someday I want to see the ocean," I told Keon as he caught up with me.

"You've never been to a real beach?" he asked, surprised.

"Nope just this," I said, gesturing to the lake.

"We'll go one day," Keon promised, and I smiled at him because even if he couldn't really make that promise, I knew he wanted to. And man, it felt good to have someone who wanted to.

We were only able to stay for a few minutes more, but something inside me did feel recharged as we left the beach. The city didn't even look quite as menacing afterward.

At least until the cemetery came into view.

Julian's "hosting" the funeral. I didn't know that was a thing but apparently because Julian was my mother's master, he paid and planned her funeral, even though he was also her murderer.

The supernatural world has its own graveyard in Chicago, just beyond the largest human one, Rosehill Cemetery. From the outside, it looks like there are just rows of skyscrapers. But if a human were to walk towards it, they would suddenly remember something urgent they needed to do. Who knew the supernatural world was responsible for helping humans to remember all the things they'd forgotten about?

However, as soon as you pass through the ward surrounding the supernatural cemetery, the illusion of the skyscrapers disappears and you find yourself in Jonestown Cemetery. Every supernatural who was anyone in Chicago was buried here. At least Julian was giving my mother that.

A shiver passed over my skin as we moved through the ward, the magic pricking at my skin like it was trying to jump into my veins. Keon acted nonplussed as we went through, and I frowned at how unaffected he seemed about most things... most things except for me.

It had been a sunny day, but passing through the wards you would never know. It was like the creators of the cemetery wanted the weather to reflect the feelings of its occupants. The sky was a stormy grey color, no sign of the sun and there was a light mist falling. The air was cooler as well, and I shivered as we began to make our way down the path that wound through the gravestones. Keon wrapped an arm around me and I snuggled into his warmth. He always seemed to be on fire.

There wasn't a sign of anyone until we walked up a hill, and then we could see the honorary red canopies set up to protect the attendees from the weather. My stomach squeezed as we got closer and I could see the hole dug in the ground. There'd been a viewing earlier. I hadn't been given details about how Julian had killed her, but evidently, it wasn't anything ghastly enough to prevent the viewing. My mother's face popped in my mind. She was beautiful, but it was a cruel beauty. Had I ever seen her give me a genuine smile? Had she smiled when I'd been born? Had she looked down at my face and felt any hint of love?

There was a crowd of people gathered under the tents. I recognized some of the other sirens, but soon noticed they weren't excited to see me. Each of them averted their eyes like they'd catch something just by looking at me. Why had I worried so much about helping them again? Their feelings were obviously not the same.

Many from Julian's clan were here as well. A lot of them had used my mother personally when she hadn't been busy with clients. Their hungry eyes followed me as Keon led me to two empty seats and I struggled not to shiver under their stares. At least I hadn't seen...no sooner had I thought it than Julian appeared from behind one of the drapes hanging off the canopies. His face lit up when he saw me, but not like Keon's did. Julian's face was lit up in the way a cat lit up when it saw a mouse.

I ignored him to stare at the casket sitting in front of the canopies. My heart beat furiously in my chest as I looked at it. It was made of dark mahogany wood. Red roses were draped over it. More blood-red roses were strewn artfully around the casket. It was gaudy and impressive and Jocelyn would have loved it. There was light classical music streaming from hidden speakers and everyone was whispering as if they were trying to be respectful of the moment.

It was such a joke.

The priest from the local church that Julian had made us attend most Sundays stood up in front of the crowd and everyone quieted down and found their seats.

"God doesn't know why some are chosen to be taken from us so soon," the priest began. Fury rushed through my veins. Fury and incredulousness that this farce was actually happening. God had nothing to do with my mother's death. Only Julian did, and he was sitting front and center on the first row, people patting his back like he had lost someone important or something.

The priest droned on and on, his gaze darting among the crowd, stopping every so often on the other sirens. He was probably thinking about his next "appointment" with one of them. I knew for a fact that Julian sent him a girl every Saturday night. The priest was no more celibate than I was.

"Julian will now grace us with a few words," the priest finally said and Keon growled next to me. For a second, I allowed myself to imagine letting the serial killer I had at my disposal lose. But I knew it wouldn't be as easy as that. Julian was a walking weapon, with many of the siren's powers at his disposal in addition to his own. Even with Keon's brutal strength, and whatever that monster was inside him, I didn't think that he would be a match for a Vampire Grand Master.

But it sure was nice to imagine.

Julian's gaze was mocking as he stared at me while he gave a glowing eulogy for my mother. The Jocelyn he described was a stranger, a lie... and he knew it. I looked around, still expecting someone to think it was ridiculous and insulting for my mother's murderer to be speaking during her funeral, but no one seemed to care. Julian finally finished and a freaking choir, that appeared out of the woodwork, began to sing some sad old song that I'd heard at funerals before.

At least it would be over soon. One of the siren girls, Kayla, walked up and down the aisles, dropping off roses to each of the guests. I guessed to place on the casket. The guests stood up and dropped the roses off one by one as Julian stood by the casket, nodding at everyone as they paid their respects.

"Maybe we should slip out now," I suggested.

"You deserve the chance to say goodbye," Keon said through gritted teeth. "He's not going to touch you."

Keon kept his hand firmly on my lower back as we

approached the casket, my rose gripped tightly in my hand. Julian's jaw clenched as he stared at Keon's familiar touch.

I pointedly ignored him, walking steadfastly to the casket and laying the rose down on top of it with the hundreds of other roses already there. My hand shook as I released the flower.

"I hope you found some peace wherever you are. Some peace... and some happiness, mama," I whispered, the old endearment from what felt like another life popping from my tongue. A flicker of a memory popped in my head as my fingers traced the wood of the coffin. A memory of her face... smiling down at me.

I let the memory sink into my skin, letting it soothe away the years of hurt and the pain. I let myself forgive her. I would never forget all she had done. But somehow, I thought that it would give the both of us, my mother and me, the peace we needed if I was able to forgive.

A smile flickered across my face.

"I've missed that pretty smile," Julian said from way too close to me, shattering the momentary feeling of peace I'd been experiencing. Keon yanked me away and pushed me behind him. I could just imagine the glare Julian was giving him.

"Hiding, Selena?" Julian asked in a voice that was supposed to sound amused, but mostly just sounded annoyed.

I huffed a deep breath and then pushed myself from behind Keon. "Hello to you too, Julian. This was a lot, even for you," I said, gesturing to his presence at the funeral.

He put on a mock sad face. "You gave me no choice.

The prison doesn't seem to be teaching you the right lessons, so I decided to help you."

I gritted my teeth to try and stop myself from saying anything in response. That's what he wanted, for me to engage. Keon lunged forward, and I caught the back of his suit coat.

"Don't," I whispered fiercely. "Let's just go."

Keon rolled his shoulders back and grabbed my hand, and we began to march past Julian. He hissed and grabbed my arm and jerked me towards him, lurching me from Keon's hand.

"You get more beautiful every day, sweetheart," he purred. "It's about time for you to be coming home, don't you think? Surely that pussy isn't too stretched out from how much use it's been getting. Maybe you've even learned some tricks from slumming it with that crime lord you're so fond of."

"What did you just say?" Keon roared. I could feel the eyes of the guests who hadn't left yet watching the scene in rapt fascination. The people of this city thrived on drama and pain, and there was plenty of it at the funeral today. I just didn't want us to become the main attraction. A funeral planned by a murderer was enough.

Julian smiled cruelly, the glimmer in his eyes telling me he was just itching for a fight. Keon's eyes began to glow and he began to shake. He was definitely about to "wolf" out so to speak. Or "demon" out. I wasn't quite sure what he was. But last time that had happened, I'd died, so I'd like to avoid that.

An image of Keon in a prison suit instead of a guard's uniform filled my head and I knew that was what Julian was going for.

"Keon, it's alright. It's just words," I whispered. "I'm fine. I'm here. We need to go." I repeated the words soothingly until the glow in his gaze faded and his shaking had stopped.

"Your time will come, asshole," Keon growled before he took my hand again, and we walked away.

I could feel Julian's disappointed stare hot on my back the whole trip away.

"I'll be coming for you, Selena. In just a few days. And no one will be able to stop me."

We kept walking even though I could feel the tension in Keon's body. It was killing him to just walk away without a fight. It was a good thing Alaric wasn't here. There'd be a lot of casualties. I wasn't sure that Alaric could match up against Julian either, but the fight would've been bloody.

"Enjoy your last few days," Julian uncharacteristically yelled at us since he wasn't getting the attention he wanted.

"Fuck you," I murmured under my breath, hoping it would carry in the wind. I started to walk faster, wanting to get Keon away before he decided to stay and fight. He was shaking again.

We made it over the hill, but I didn't start really breathing again until we'd made it past the wards and we were back in the sunshine of the city once again.

Hatred clogged in my gut, muting the bright colors of the day. I felt worn out, demolished from the emotion of the day.

"I hate that fucker," Keon growled. "He's never going to get you back," he swore fiercely, grabbing my face in his hands and leveling me with a kiss that had me reeling.

He looked beautiful with the sunlight falling across his features. I still wasn't used to the sight. The prison lights just didn't quite have the same effect.

"Someday I'm going to get my power back," I swore to him. "Someday."

Keon squeezed my hand. He'd heard me say that before.

I just wish we both believed it.

CHAPTER 2

KEON

I was the first to admit I had a dark heart. I didn't have time for others, didn't give a shit about most things... but then Selene had waltzed into the bar and stole more than my attention. She grabbed my heart and wrenched it out of my chest. This beautiful girl was everything to me. For her, I would burn down the whole world if it would make her smile.

And now... well now my heart was shattering for her and there wasn't a fucking thing I could do about it. Her agony tore me up each time I looked into her red-teary eyes, at the way she tried to hold back the waterworks. I'd shown her the real me, told her about the demonic monster inside me, even that I had to keep feeding it souls, and she remained by my side. My whole body shuddered at the knowledge that she might be the first person who had ever accepted me as I was and still wanted to get close. My mind raced with the recent events, with how much I needed to viciously murder, Julian, all while I tried to maneuver around Chicago traffic which was a bitch on the best of days.

My beast bellowed in my head that I ought to hunt down Julian tonight, to skin him alive. But I was also aware that there was much more at play here than just him. The problem was that killing him wouldn't release my gorgeous girl from prison, and she didn't want to run away, so for a change, I needed to use my head to sort this mess out.

Taking in deep breaths, I looked over to my beauty, who was curled in on herself in the passenger seat next to me in her black dress, the long sleeves loose, and the low round neck showing a hint of cleavage. She had the window open, and the cool hair billowed through her hair.

Mine, my beast snarled in my chest. *All mine.*

And I couldn't agree more.

"I have a surprise for you," I told her, reaching over and placing a hand on her thigh, my fingers finding the warm spark of her skin. Nightmare Penitentiary procedure dictated that I had to have her locked up in the back seat, handcuffed to the door, but that wasn't going to happen.

She twisted away from the window and lifted her head toward me. Fresh tears balanced on the edges of her eyes, and she offered me a lopsided grin. "What is it?"

"We have a bit of extra time before we have to return to the penitentiary, so I want to take you somewhere."

She stared at me, not responding right away, and I couldn't tell if she might cry again. In all honesty, it was destroying me to see her cry. After I had killed her accidentally back in the prison, I had been on the verge of losing all control, of going so batshit crazy that I doubted I'd ever find myself again. Now, I clung to her like a desperate man finally finding his purpose in life. It sounded sappy, but I didn't give a fuck when I only cared about what happened to her.

She swiped the back of her hand under an eye, catching a loose tear. "Oh yeah, where's that?"

"That's a surprise."

She glanced out the front window at the road we were crawling along. "I used to hate traffic," she murmured. "But I miss it, just like I miss the simple things. The birds in the trees, families laughing, or cute dogs on leashes on the sidewalk with their owners. I miss the basic stuff I barely noticed before."

Heartache shook her words, and I squeezed her thigh slightly to let her know I was there for her. Without a word, she leaned against my side, and I looped an arm around her waist. I thought about how I'd like to scoop her up and press her inside me, to keep her protected from the rest of the world.

She closed her eyes and I held her tightly as I wove my way through the city. The radio played a soft tune in the background, something I didn't recognize, but offered a calming effect from the honking outside.

It was only once we left behind the city and I turned down a side street that Selena opened her eyes. She straightened, asking, "Where are we?"

I eased off the gas pedal as we cruised down a street with only four houses, each boasting plenty of land and privacy on either side between each of their neighbors'. I came to a stop in front of a single-family home with a dark limestone facade. Two-story with a pointy roof, black-framed arched windows, complete with a metal fence out the front for the perfect, normal home.

"Whose house is this?" she asked, looking at me and back to the property.

"It's my place."

Her mouth dropped, then she unbuckled her seatbelt and climbed out of the car for an even better look. "It's spectacular and not quite what I imagined for you."

I got out and joined her, laughing as it was exactly why I selected this home. To remain inconspicuous. "It's private enough, comes with a lot of empty land that backs up to a forest, and even a graveyard."

Her expression that time had me laughing louder.

"Ah, okay, well that kind of makes more sense then."

"The cemetery was purely coincidental," I explained.

"It's huge, and you live here alone?"

"For now, yes." I didn't mention that the house comes with a massive, locked basement for when my beast needs to emerge and I can't control him.

She tilted her head to the side and stared at me with admiration like somehow her impression of me had changed by just knowing I owned a house. While my heart pounded in my chest at how hard it was for me to take her back to prison.

"Want to see the inside?"

"Yes!" Her response came fast, her eyes gleaming with excitement.

In seconds, we passed through the front door, and she rushed ahead of me into the main living room. Her shoes tapping on the wooden floorboards as she moved. She paused and spun on the spot, taking it all in. For a few moments, I let myself imagine what it might be like living with her in this house, and with it came an unbearable need so heavy it was close to breaking me. I couldn't remember a time in my life when I felt this close to anyone.

"I don't have much furniture," I told her as she ran her hand across the back of the black, leather sofa facing the flat-screen TV on the wall. There was also a fireplace, but that was it in this room. I was a minimalist mostly because I spent more time at the penitentiary in my room there than I did at home.

I gave her the grand tour of my house, including the basement which she didn't question, then we both headed out into the backyard on the patio. The land stretched out to a dense line of trees in the distance, and Selena continued to walk towards the overgrown lawn. I often come and sit out here in the middle of the night, losing myself to the wilderness in my mind.

"It's so calm here," Selena murmured, strolling forward while kicking off her shoes and leaving them behind.

The wind tossed her dark hair over her shoulders, the sunlight beaming against the blue tips. There was so much innocence in just the way she moved through the grass. I tried hard to ignore the tightening in my chest at how quickly I'd fallen for her.

Her dress hugged her body, following her hourglass waist and the curve of her gorgeous ass, while my gaze lingered on her long, toned legs. She stopped and looked up, closing her eyes, letting the sun heat her face.

She was spectacular.

It was true what they said about *the higher you build walls around your heart, the harder you fall when someone tore them down.*

I needed to stop overthinking everything, so I made my way to Selene while leaving my shoes behind me, the soil cold beneath my feet.

Selena lowered her head and turned to face me. As if on cue, her nipples tightened and pushed against the material of her dress in my presence.

"You are incredible," I said and captured her in my arms, lifting her off her feet.

"Thank you for everything," she whispered while her hands slid around my neck, tender fingers threading through my hair.

We stayed like that for a long time, looking into each other's eyes, and while I couldn't tell what she was thinking, she didn't want me to let her go either.

"Why are you so nice to me, when..." Her words die off, but she didn't shy away. There was something brazen about her today, something raw and primal.

"When I'm a monster on the inside?" I finished her sentence.

She shrugged but didn't try to backtrack on her words. I've tried to avoid the thoughts and doubts that she might change her mind about being with someone like me.

"You see me for who I am and haven't run away. I had thought about how to tell you about the real me for a long time, afraid you would no longer love me if you saw who I truly was."

"That's where you were very wrong." But before I could respond, she leaned toward me, gripping the sides of my head, and was kissing me. Her legs curling around my waist, her body wrapped around me so beautifully.

I growled my desire and need under my breath, my hands

cupping her ass as I kissed her back with the ferociousness she delivered. If this was what she needed to forget the shitty funeral, if she needed me to be the guy she used to let go of everything, then I'd let her have me as she craved.

"My whole life I've been surrounded by monsters," she whispered against my mouth. "They took everything from me. So no, you're not a monster, Keon. You are the demon I fell for, the demon who will slay every last monster in my life."

Her words are my addiction, and for her, I would kill anyone she asks. "My mother once told me that when you fall in love, you do so with the little things about someone. Like how I adore the way you laugh, the way you smell like candy, how your eyes glow and mouth forms into a smile each time you see me."

"Well, if we are confessing, I was terrified at first to want you. You are an intimidating person. And yet, here I am, wrapped in your arms, wanting you regardless."

I fucking loved her. My hands slid under her thighs, finding bare skin. My mouth parted to respond, to say something, but no words came out. I wasn't normally lost in emotions, but at that moment, I was too far gone.

"I'm sorry your life is screwed up. But I will never leave your side." A sense of weightlessness flared over me, and I kissed her. Gently, I fell to my knees and laid her onto her back on the grass, concealing us from the neighbors in the far distance. Then I followed, laying my body over hers.

"I need you, Keon. Here. Now."

"I know, and you have all of me." My mouth watered at the thought of claiming her, and I slid a hand up the side of her thigh. I curled two fingers under the elastic of her underwear and ripped them off her easily.

She gasped and giggled while tugging my shirt up and out of my pants. I pushed back onto my heels to undo my belt and her sweet scent filled my lungs. With it came all the dirty things I wanted to do with and to her, if I could steal her away from the world.

A quick glance around confirmed we were still alone and none of the neighbors were about. I grinned as I pushed down my pants. She was quick to lean in and take my heavy cock in her tiny hand.

I hissed at the softness of her fingers curling around me, the firmness of her grip. The desperation to feel her touch had my cock twitching in her palm. I pushed her skirt up, needing to see her wet pussy, and when I ran a finger along the seam, she moaned. I licked my lips at the way her body responded, at her falling back down on the lawn, her hips rising and falling for me.

I pushed myself between her thighs and laid back on top of her, my hands holding the sides of her head, and I kissed her with a passion I never wanted her to forget.

"Please, Keon," she whispered, pivoting her pelvis to reach my erection. She kissed me with fire, and any control I thought I held dissolved beneath my hunger for her.

Pressing a palm to the ground beside her shoulder, I took her wrist and placed it over her head, then I did the same with the other. She was so small that I easily clasped both her wrists in one hand, holding them in place. She stared up at me, her expression one of vulnerability and desire, one where she'd given herself over to me. She was my drug, and I could never give her up. And I have her exactly where I'd wanted her.

I sucked in harsh, rapid breaths, barely holding onto any control because of how insanely I wanted her. Not much scared me, but the effect she had on me did.

"I've missed you," she whispered, sincerity flashing in her eyes. "When I'm not with you, I can't stop thinking of the way you fuck me."

I shuddered in response, and I pressed my cock into her drenched pussy, unable to hold back.

She moaned, and the way her chest arched upward in response destroyed me. A sharp ache settles beneath my heart, one that told me I was too far gone for Selena, to the point that our relationship could only end in two ways. She was mine for eternity, or one of us died.

"I adore your body." I groan under my breath. I push deeper into her tight core. And kiss her, my mouth sliding down to her neck, nibbling on her flesh. "My sweet, gorgeous girl." Grazing my teeth over her neck, I drove myself completely into her. She cries out, and I bite down into her neck. Not hard enough to break the skin, but enough to leave my mark, to proclaim my dominance, to appease my beast.

She wriggled beneath me, but never pushed me away. Instead, she demanded more. I moved my hips, working her faster, igniting the fire between us. She stuck out her chest, her breasts against me, her nipples hard.

I let go of her wrists and roughly pulled at the neckline of her dress, tugging her bra down and finding myself the perfect cherry teasing me. I closed my mouth around her nipple, sucking hard while fucking her. Being buried deep inside her was a mixed sensation of heaven and hell... one

I lost myself in, but also couldn't get enough of. She had played on my mind constantly, her naked body imprinted in my memory. But the moments I claimed her were everything to me.

Delicious moans sang in my ears as I dragged my erection against her walls, and she was suddenly screaming. My beauty quivered against me, bursting with an orgasm. This was what I'd been craving. The arousal deep inside me intensified, rising to the surface as I thrust into her harder. I dropped a hand to her waist and swooped my arm under her back, and I pulled her in harder against my body.

I growled, my climax hitting as hard as hers. I hissed, tensed, and roared. Our bodies intertwined and locked together. We were one.

Selena remained caged beneath me, while my beast snarled in my chest, already demanding more even as I pumped my seed into her.

When we finally quietened down, she flopped her head back on the ground, smiling wickedly. We were both covered in sweat, her neck bright red from my bite, and the air perfumed with her addictive scent. We laid together, with me still buried in her, I wasn't ready to leave her yet.

"You are everything," she whispered to me. "And I need more. Stop holding out on me."

I kissed her chin and her lips, then skimmed a thumb across her cheek. The agony in her eyes burned me like scorching fire licking at my insides. "You belong to me and if I had my way, I'd keep you in my bed every single night." My heart thundered in my chest, feeling like it might burst free when I thought about taking her back to prison.

"Me too," she murmured. "Part of me stupidly wants you to take me away now, so we don't have to ever return to where I will never see the sun again. To be locked up forever." She frowned and turned her head to the side, staring out into the distance at the water, lost in the reality of how fucked up her situation truly was. That the short moments of reprieve I just gave her aren't enough to deal with a lifetime in prison.

My breathing picked up, and it cut me deeply to see her that low. But her plea for help wasn't missed. I slipped a hand under her neck and lifted her head to face me. She blinked, her sweet mouth parting to say something, but her words were stolen by me.

"I'll make you a promise, Selena. I will find a way to get you out of the Nightmare Penitentiary. I'll fuck up everything in our path to make it happen. Okay?"

She nodded, not speaking, but the glistening in her gaze showed me the desperation she clung to for an escape. In front of me was a woman staring at me like I just offered her the answer to all her problems. I slowly swept my mouth over hers, running my tongue over her sweet lips, intending to make her forget her worries at least one more time before we returned.

CHAPTER 3

SELENA

I didn't realize how much it would suck to come back to Nightmare Penitentiary. I mean obviously, I realized it wouldn't be fun to get a taste of freedom and then find myself back in hell. But the dread I was experiencing at the moment went far beyond anything I could have comprehended.

I knew what was waiting for me now. The dim hallways, the cacophony of screams that never ended. And the fights any time you stepped outside your cell. I shivered as I walked beside Keon, wishing he was allowed to touch me. Already I missed him. The short time we shared outside the prison, at his home, meant the world to me. They were memories locked in my mind to keep me going for as long as possible in this rotten place.

But he couldn't, not in here in front of everyone. The other guards were watching us closely. I had to pretend he was no one to me once again.

"It'll be okay," Keon whispered to me under his breath

"""

as we passed through the same gates I'd entered months before.

"Yeah," I murmured, as the doors slid open. I could already hear the screams, I wanted to run as far away as I could.

Why hadn't I taken up Keon's offer to run away?

Right. Because I was an idiot.

We'd only made it a little way down one of the hallways when another guard approached us. Keon stiffened as he got closer. I knew he was trying to withhold the urge to tell the guy to fuck off. Or maybe even kill him. I'm sure he was itching for violence after not being able to do anything to Julian.

"The Warden's expecting you," the guard announced with a smug smirk. Keon's grip tightened on my arm.

"We just got back from her mother's funeral. Surely, the Warden isn't expecting her now?" Keon growled.

The guard's smirk grew. "He wants her now, and you know that it will be worse for her if he has to wait."

Keon opened his mouth, then closed it, as if he didn't know what to say. And what could he say? He knew that there was nothing we could do. In this place, the Warden was king, and there was nothing we could do to change that.

Dread curdled in my gut. How was it possible that no matter where I was, I always felt powerless? That didn't change whether I was inside or outside these walls.

"I'll take her," Keon announced, but the guard was already shaking his head before Keon had finished speaking.

"There's a fight brewing in the northern quadrant. The

Warden heard rumors of it from one of his informants, and he wants extra guards over there. That includes you."

Keon was trembling again and frankly; I didn't have the energy to deal with the fallout that would occur if something happened with the guard.

"Sounds good," I chirped to the guard, walking away from Keon before he could do anything.

Keon's anger trailed after me as I hurried past the guard in the direction that I thought the Warden's office was. The halls were always changing in this place. It was impossible to keep track of where it was even though I'd been called there often enough that you would think I'd have it figured out by now.

I shot a look over my shoulder as I walked, hoping that Keon could read the apology in my eyes. Distress was written all over his features, and I wondered how long this could go on before Keon messed up and we were found out. I needed to do my best to make sure that didn't happen. I couldn't take messing up anyone else's life. My mother losing hers because of me had been enough.

The walk to the Warden's office took forever, but the guard was blissfully quiet. I hadn't seen that creepy guard again, and I kind of wondered if he hadn't been "dealt with" by either Keon or Alaric. A smile slid across my face. I'm sure it looked demented. This place was really changing me.

I took a deep breath when we finally got there, steeling myself for whatever fresh torture the Warden had in store for me. I wished I knew why he seemed to have it out for me. I hadn't gotten the feeling that he and Julian were besties, but there didn't seem to be another reason for the delight he got in putting me through the wringer.

The Warden was sitting behind his giant desk writing something when I walked into the room. I hovered near a chair, waiting for him to acknowledge me. My gaze couldn't help but flick to the orb on the bookshelf filled with my power. Every cell in my body yearned to be reunited with it.

It felt like a piece of me was existing away from my body. I could picture in my mind how it had felt to have it reunited with me... how it had felt to be whole.

I heard a snort and looked over to see the Warden shaking his head at the piece of paper on his desk. With a sigh, he set his pen down and finally gave me his attention, though obviously, he'd known I'd been waiting in front of him this whole time.

"Enjoy your field trip?" he asked cheerily as if I'd been on a jaunt to the zoo instead of my mother's fucking funeral.

I said nothing, knowing that he was just goading me. I bit the inside of my cheek so hard to keep from saying something that I tasted blood.

The Warden grinned like a cat who'd just caught the canary. Seriously, what the hell was wrong with this guy? I really hoped that someone gave him a piece of his own medicine someday. Even better if that person was me.

"I just got a call from your Master," he said flippantly.

More blood gushed into my mouth at that announcement... and of the Warden's use of the word "master."

"Seems like the asshole has missed you. You must have made quite the impression on him at the funeral. He's coming in the next few weeks to take you back home."

"No!" The word burst out of my mouth before I could stop it. I hadn't really expected Julian to follow through with his threat, and especially not this quickly. I thought for sure I'd hurt his pride too much for him to want me out of here.

I was not going back to him, that was for sure. I would rather die.

"You'd rather stay here?" the Warden asked with a grin. "I wasn't aware that I was running such hospitable accommodations. I'll have to check in with the staff. They seem to be slacking in their jobs if that's how my guests feel."

"With all due respect, I'm all for getting released, sir. But I will not be going back home."

"And what makes you think that you would be released for any reason other than Julian deciding to give you leniency, little girl?" he purred dangerously.

"Because I'm innocent," I spit out, not sure where this courage was coming from, and not sure if this was actually courage or me being an idiot.

I was inclined to think it was the latter.

The Warden leaned forward over his desk, his hands clasped together in front of him like we were talking about vacation plans or something like that. "What would your innocence have to do with anything?" he asked with an evil grin.

Rage coursed through me. "You know I'm fucking innocent, you monster," I screeched. Red flashed in my vision and I lost control over myself. I picked up a paperweight on his desk and threw it blindly at one of his bookshelves filled with his precious heirlooms. I was so sick of this motherfucker.

The paperweight smashed through the fragile glass shelves of the bookcase, destroying everything in its path. And I watched in horror as everything fell to the floor, shattering on impact with a deafening roar as glass, and gemstones, and who knows what else went flying through the air.

As the rage left my body, horror settled in.

The silence after everything stopped moving was deafening. The Warden stared at me in shock before his gaze turned to the carnage I'd just created in his office.

I was shaking as I watched his reaction. What the hell had I just done? The Warden started to flicker in and out, his form disappearing into the black mists that I'd sworn I'd seen in the past. Rage filled the air, so thick I could almost taste it. The mist began to stretch and expand until it was hard to see my hand in front of my face. And the temperature dropped so low in the room that I was shaking not only from fear but from the cold itself.

"I-." I tried to apologize, but the words died in my throat. There was nothing I could say to make what I'd just done go away. He was probably going to take me to Julian right now just to get rid of me and make sure I was punished thoroughly.

The mists swirled around the room, and it was easy to believe that the rumors about him were true at this moment. How he embodied a nightmare.

The mists continued to stretch until the room was now black as night. Hopelessness seeped into my skin, and it felt like my life would be over at any moment.

Just before I'd lost all hope, the mists snapped back into the Warden, as sudden as if they were a rubber band.

As terrifying as the mists had been, the Warden was somehow even more terrifying in his regular form. He stared at me with a withering look of utter contempt, like he was imagining me dying in a thousand gruesome ways.

"You will be released to Julian," he said in a cold, cruel voice. "If you manage to survive..."

"If I manage to survive?" I asked in a choked voice.

"I've placed a bounty on your head. As we speak, it's being announced to every one of the psycho scum that resides in these hallowed halls. You won't manage a moment of peace during the rest of your time here. You won't sleep, you won't be able to eat, you will never be safe." He gave me a smile that was all teeth and I swore I could see the devil in his gaze as his stare bore down on me. "I hope your temper tantrum was worth it."

A burst of wind followed his deadly statement, and I was pushed out of his office and flung against one of the stone walls, my head snapping back and hitting the stone so hard I almost blacked out. I was left feeling woozy and out of sorts.

I fell forward on my knees and began to dry heave from the concussion he'd just given me. I would rather die than fall into Julian's hands again.

But this hadn't been what I was thinking.

A pair of guard's boots stepped into my vision, and I looked up at the sneering guard standing above me knowingly.

I was so fucked.

CHAPTER 4

SELENA

I'd been called back to the mess hall to work the next day. Apparently, they had been under-staffed, and somehow that was my fault because now I had to pull double shifts. But after my encounter with the Warden, I wanted to lock myself up in my cell. Every person I saw terrified me.

I hated this place and nearly everyone in it. The only thing that kept me sane were the four men in my life, but could they really keep me safe? As complicated and dangerous as they were, they belonged to me. All night, I held onto Keon's promise that he'd find a way to get me out permanently. I couldn't even fathom how that was possible, but I clung to that thread of hope like my life depended on it. And it definitely did.

A new guard stood outside the mess hall, staring at me, waiting for me to hurry up with getting the meal cart prepared so we could begin our shift. He looked at me like I was a speck of dirt, and even from across the room, I hated him. I could only imagine that the Warden had put him on my delivery schedule to make my life hell.

Maybe it was my mother's death, the encounter with Julian, or the threat from the Warden, but I'd lost my patience somewhere over the last couple of days.

I dumped the last two trays of meals on my cart and started pushing it across the mess hall. The morning run was always uneventful as most locked inmates remained asleep.

The guard with beady eyes grunted at me, and I loathed him even more if that was possible. Then we were off, and I was rushing to keep up because apparently, he didn't care that I had shorter legs than him or that I was pushing a packed cart with meals jiggling about that took some maneuvering.

It wasn't long before we reached the far end of the next floor down... the place where they kept some of the semi-dangerous inmates. It wasn't complete isolation down here, not like the pits down below and across the bridge of what can only be called Hell. This was what I liked to call the seedy part.

Inmates wandered past us, eyeing me up and down, staring at the cart as one of the wheels kept squeaking.

We turned the corner to a long corridor so long I couldn't see the end from here. Though, it could be the number of people blocking my view. The last guard and I usually moved quickly through this section.

"Off you go," the guard ordered.

I glanced up at him, perplexed. "Aren't you supposed to accompany all my deliveries?"

He yawned, then leaned a shoulder against the wall. "I

can see you from here." He stuck his hand into his pocket and pulled out his cell phone before tapping it.

Right. So, he was too lazy to walk down the massive corridor. Asshole. Yet my legs wouldn't move, not when the Warden's warning blared in my mind. "If someone attacks me for the meals, it's your fault."

He barked a laugh. "As if anyone would want to steal that slop."

My shoulders pinched backward at his insult, seeing as the meals are the same ones I was enjoying for breakfast too.

His eyebrows shot up, staring at me. "Tick-tock, the meals won't deliver themselves. Now, get going."

If my gaze could skewer someone to the wall, he'd be a shish kebab already.

Settling on not letting his assholeness get to me and praying to whoever was looking over me to keep me safe, I lifted my chin, spun on my heels, and pushed the cart down the long passage.

Of course, each time I glanced back over my shoulder, he wasn't watching me. I could be kidnapped and taken into someone's cell, and he'd be none the wiser. I preferred the old guard.

Except, I shouldn't expect anything else in this shithole.

The squealing wheel grabbed peoples' attention, but luckily for me, most were still half asleep to really be bothered to do anything about me being in their block.

The first locked door I came on, I knocked twice. "Mealtime," I called out, then grabbed a food tray and slipped it through the food slot. Like I said, these weren't the most dangerous, so these tiny hatches weren't locked up. I could just imagine it helped with other inmates passing them all kinds of contraband. The guy behind the door grunted, and the next thing I knew, the tray was tugged from my hands. The metal flap flopped back down. Okay, someone was hungry. I kept going on my delivery route.

In all honesty, I didn't know how I managed to survive in the penitentiary so long, but I was definitely a different girl from the one thrown in here months ago. But now, I kept frantically staring at anyone I passed, anyone that might suddenly attack me unprovoked to do the Warden's bidding.

Toward the end of the hallway, I reached the final door, and when I glanced back the way I'd come, I could barely make out the guard. But it was clear even from here, he still had his face shoved in that damn phone. A shiver zipped up my spine from how vulnerable I felt.

I looked back at him still tapping his phone, and I grit my teeth. He was probably ordering himself a blow-up doll because it was the only kind of woman who'd be interested in him. I sniggered to myself and turned to collect the next food tray when a whimpering sound came from the shadows of the hallway.

Before I got a chance to make sense of what I was seeing, a woman recoiled backward in my direction, her wrists tied behind her back, her short, blond hair messy. Her orange overalls had one arm completely torn off, the thing hanging by a few threads from her wrist.

My mind spun on what I was looking at, and what she was doing. Was this some sexual roleplay thing I'd stumbled onto?

But when she twisted her head toward me, reality

punched me. Tape covered her mouth, and her tearful, terrified eyes clashed with mine. Trepidation paled her face. My heart hit the back of my throat because she was in danger, and that idiot guard was nowhere close for me to call out to him.

She moaned at me, her green eyes massive, and I stilled at first, unsure where to turn next to help her. Movement caught my eye from a cell behind her.

A man, at least six-five, stepped out of the shadows, black hair, tangled with what looked like dark feathers. He wore no shirt and wasn't exactly bulky, but the look in his eyes terrified me.

I read somewhere once that when you looked into a predator's eyes, you knew right away you were in danger. And right then, I felt like I'd just walked into a wolf's den, and the beast was starved.

I lost my breath, while the poor girl whimpered, stumbling toward me. The few inmates that had been around us scrambled out of there because they knew a monster lived down there.

He sucked in a breath, making a slurpy wet sound, and I hated that my first thought flew to Hannibal Lecter from The Silence Of The Lambs.

"Fuck!" the word fell from my lips.

"Oh, my sparrow, you have found me another girl. One who has angered the Warden too…so another set of eyes for me it is. How exciting." His gaze widened, studying my face when the glint of something drew my attention to the small, hooked blade in his hand.

I screamed purely out of instinct, while my hands gripped the cart that stood between him and us.

Looking back quickly, of course, no one came to our

rescue, and the guard didn't move. I was going to murder him if I got out of this alive.

"He's not coming for you, my little finch." He makes that horrible sound again that makes me gag.

I doubted I'd get far if I ran, and could I live with myself at leaving this poor terrified girl at his mercy?

My fingers curled around the plastic spork on the cart, knowing that it wasn't much of a weapon, but I'd make it work. Instead of panicking, I lifted my gaze to the man.

"Don't come near us. The guard will be in seconds," I said with bravery I barely believed in. I had no idea what to expect from him, but I'd been in enough fights in here to have picked up a few things on surviving.

The girl next to me was moaning behind the gag, pushing her tied-up hands against my side to untie her.

"Don't even think about it," he threatened, lifting his blade. "I'm not asking for much. You each give me one of your eyes, and I'll let you both go. Now, let's start, I'm starved."

I might have just peed my pants... just a tiny bit, I was shaking that much. Where the heck was Keon or Alaric, or even Laz?

"Get. The. Fuck. Away. From. Us!" I enunciated every word to drive my message home, to show him I wasn't weak.

But the grin curling on his thin mouth didn't reassure me in the slightest that I'd succeeded. Not when a shiver crawled up my spine.

He advanced on us, and I recoiled, dragging the meal cart to keep something between us, the girl glued to my side. My mind was whirling with what to do next.

But instead of freaking out and waiting for someone to help us, I did the next best thing.

I shoved the cart with all my strength at the guy, then grabbed the girl's arm, and whipped us around. Then we were running like our lives depended on it, which they did.

A crash boomed from the cart falling over.

Terror jolted up my legs, a scream in my throat as we continued to move. Inmates from up ahead; looked at us, but no one came to our rescue, and that fucking guard didn't even crane his neck to look up. I released that scream, but he was too far to hear it.

Something hard struck my shoulder, and suddenly, I was wrenched backward, my feet giving out from under me.

Terror squeezed my heart as I hit the floor hard. The girl lost her footing too, falling face-first, and I winced for her.

Scrambling back around, a shadow fell over me. The guy stood there, wings extending out from his back on either side of him. They were covered in feathers as black as a raven's, his irises, turning black as well.

I lost all ability to think straight as I rushed to my feet, my heart thundering in my ears. He lifted his blade, and everything about him reminded me of a bird... He was a fucking bird shifter.... raven more specifically. Then I remembered a story I'd once heard of a raven shifter serial killer leaving behind dead bodies, their eyes removed.

Instantly, I reached down and grabbed the girl by the arm, hauling her to her feet.

"Look," I said to the shifter. "I don't want any trouble.

Leave us alone and you won't receive a visit later from Keon and Alaric."

Something crossed his face at the sound of their names, but just as quickly the look vanished. "Send them to me, little finch. I will be ready."

Fuck!

We were backing away from him when he came at me so fast, I barely saw him move. Instinct took over, and I shoved the girl out of his reach, then ducked under his arm as he came flying toward me. I kicked my leg out wildly and slammed my heel right into his barefoot.

He groaned, making a squawking sound, but he didn't stop. So, I spun back around, my arm with the spork flying at his face. The plastic pointy ends puncturing his neck, the snap of the weapon echoing as it fell apart in my hand.

"You bitch." His hand flew backward, striking me across the side of my head. The pain radiated through my skull, and I stumbled backward as stars danced in my vision. The guy was grasping the side of his neck where I'd broken skin and drawn blood.

I crashed into the girl who hadn't run away for some reason.

She murmured louder, turning for me to undo the ribbon tying her wrists. I reached down to do just that when a squeak came from my feet and my attention shifted to my little mouse.

What was he doing here?

He was holding a gold coin between his teeth, and I had no idea where he came from. But I understood instantly. Ravens loved shiny things, they collected them, even eyes to eat it seemed, so maybe this could work.

Rapidly, I grabbed the coin from his mouth. "Thank you, little guy," I whispered and without really thinking how to do this, I hurled the gold coin at the approaching monster.

The coin struck him in the middle of the chest and bounced back down, clanging against the stone floor. His gaze followed the golden coin, and for a split second, I believed this would work. But all hope faded when he squawked out in laughter. "You think that a worthless offering will satisfy me?"

His gaze darkened, and panic gripped me. I leaned in close to the girl. "Run," I told her, my hands falling to her back, tugging at the ribbon binding her wrists. "Run for your life."

Raw fear zipped through me, the kind where deep inside I saw my own death, where I couldn't foresee how the hell I was going to get out of this intact.

"Get the fuck over here and kneel to your god!" he screeched.

But both of us were already running. I hadn't managed to fully free her arms, but we'd lost all ability to wait.

Run or be tortured were our only options.

My feet hit the ground, inmates flying out of our way on seeing us coming. Not to mention the shadowing falling over us, the black wings darkening our world.

My heart beat so fast, I was convinced I would die before he got a chance to catch me.

The girl ran for her life too, her shoulders swinging back and forth in her awkward run as her wrists remained tied behind her back.

My eyes were locked on the damn guard who still

seemed like a world away, still so far my screams wouldn't reach him.

Sharp talons dug into my back suddenly, breaking the skin, the pain excruciating. I cried out, falling forward. All I saw was my death flashing before me. How the next funeral to be held would be mine.

Hitting the hard floor on my hands and knees, I lost sight of everyone else. My sight feathered at the edges from pure dread.

I frantically turned around when a tremendously huge black raven hovered over me. Gone was the man as he'd transformed into his shifter form. And right now, curved claws like knives were coming right for my face. Black beady eyes held my gaze as if capturing me under a hypnotic spell.

I couldn't look away, couldn't move. But the terrifying scream falling from my mouth echoed through my skull.

It all happened so fast. The beast was coming for my eyes, swooping down.

Next thing I knew, electricity slammed into the bird's chest. White lines of energy wrapped around him so fast. I was still screaming.

Unleashed from whatever he'd done to hold me in place, I scrambled backward. The raven crashed into a wall then fell to the floor, the lines of electricity tightening in around him, squeezing the sheer life out of him.

The bruning stench of what was happening to him flooded the air.

A split second. That was all it took for the psychotic bird shifter to attack me and be tossed backward. A pop sounded, so loud I flinched, still sitting on my ass, watching in utter shock.

One moment, the bird squawked and fought the magic restraints, next it burst into nothing. A shower of black feathers raining down into a pile in the middle of the hallway.

I couldn't move, couldn't breathe as my brain tried to catch up to what I'd just witnessed.

Only when I turned away did I notice the girl I'd saved standing behind me with her hands pointed toward the pile of feathers, magic dancing on the tips of her fingers.

She looked down at me and lowered her arms, a red marking where the tape had covered her mouth. "I'm Nova. You saved me and for that, I owe you."

I blinked at her, wanting to say, I was saving myself as much as her, but those words never came. "How did you do that?"

Climbing to my feet, I noticed the guard was marching toward us, his face pale as a ghost. Fucking bastard. Of course, he showed up now after I almost died.

My heart was still pounding in my chest a million miles a minute. "I'm Selena. What are you?" I asked.

She laughed and ran a hand through her messy hair. "I'm kind of a wizard, but my powers aren't as powerful as they are on the outside, you know."

"They looked incredibly impressive to me just then."

Her gaze flicked to the feathers. "That fucking ass had it coming."

"Son of a bitch!" The guard skidded to a stop next to us, his attention on the shifter's remains, then he looked at Nova and me. "What the hell did you do?" he barked at us.

"Are you kidding me?" I snapped back, still shaking too

hard to tone it back. "You were too damn lazy to do your job and it almost got us killed."

He walked over to the feathers, calling in the incident on his earpiece. Swinging back toward us, he growled. "Get back to your cell," he commanded Nova. Then turned to me, grabbed my arm, and hauled me back down the hallway.

"Selena," Nova called out. "I'll be seeing you around."

But I never got the chance to respond because the dumbhead guard dragged me farther away from the scene of the crime.

"This is what's going to happen," he hisses between clenched teeth. "I'll take you back to your cell where you will spend the rest of the day. My report will outline that we were both attacked. When it comes to the bird-brain back there who's dead, we never saw a thing about it. Understood? I can make your life very uncomfortable here if you choose otherwise."

Anger flared in my chest since I was no longer the girl that assholes walked over. I'd had enough of everything, so I ripped my arm out of his grasp and turned toward him. I also noted that with him freaking out, he had no clue about the Warden's target on my back.

"Don't touch me. You can't do anything to me, I know bigger and badder monsters in this place than you could ever imagine. And they will skin you alive when they hear you put me in danger." I breathed heavily, my muscles tense, and I stared him dead straight in the eyes. I had no idea if he knew the men I associated with, but when he gave no response, I guessed he must have known.

The moment he swallowed loudly and dropped his gaze, I knew I had him.

"Lucky for you," I continued. "I don't want any of this shit to come back on me either. So, I'll say nothing, and you will never be with me on my shift again. If you see me in the prison, you fuck off in the opposite direction. Do you understand?"

He swallowed hard and glanced back toward the remains of the raven shifter. I had no idea if he witnessed Nova taking out the psycho, but if not, I'd let him believe it might have been me that had done it.

He growled his disapproval under his breath, but also didn't say a thing. "Move, I'll take you back to your cell. I have to clean up this shit."

"That's what I thought," I answered and followed him back to my cell, desperately wanting to be alone so I could finally freak out about what just happened.

CHAPTER 5

SELENA

The Warden was a man of his word...at least when it came to threats. Five days had passed since he'd placed the bounty on me and every day there had been some kind of torment. The attack from the raven shifter had been just the beginning.

I was already tired, and it hadn't even been a week.

And I'd had to go through it all alone. I hadn't seen any of the guys, even Keon, since everything had begun. We'd thought that the Warden didn't know about the relationships we were pursuing, but he had to. That was the only reason I could think of for why I hadn't seen any of them.

I wasn't an idiot. I might have kept secrets in the past, but in this situation, where anything and everyone was trying to kill me, I would have gladly told the guys everything in the hopes they could help keep me alive. I'd even been removed from the dinner rotation in the sector that would have taken me past Seth's cell. I'd been cut off from anyone who could help me.

Today that had to change, though. Somehow, I was

going to find a way to talk to one of them. If I didn't, I wasn't sure I would survive tomorrow. There were a lot of baddies in this place, a lot of creatures I hadn't even heard of... that I didn't want to hear of. There had been one yesterday that had oozed slime, and that tried to throw it at me. The slime caused extreme burns. I'd been lucky to escape with only a slight burn on my leg. Apparently, gelatinous creatures didn't move very fast because I'd been able to run away, and it hadn't been able to catch me.

I peeked around the corner, trying to use my cart as a mirror to see if anyone was lying in wait. The other day, I'd been jumped in the shower. A demon had come at me with some kind of glass shank. I was just lucky that the hot water had been turned on in the prison that day. Most of the time, the showers were ice-cold. I'd flipped the water to the hottest setting and burned the ever-loving shit out of my attacker. Since then, I hadn't slept at all remembering her screams.

I'd never imagined what I would be capable of once backed into a corner. It was terrifying to think about, actually.

My makeshift mirror didn't show anyone lying in wait, so I pushed the cart around the corner, stopping every time I heard a sound... which meant I stopped constantly. It meant that it took forever to make my meal deliveries now that they forced me to do them on my own, and I'm sure the prisoners were starving by the time they got their food. I didn't feel too bad though; they were the ones that were trying to kill me.

I made it through the first section without incident. I could see the yearning in the prisoners' eyes to come at me, but luckily their cell doors were locked, and they couldn't. A shiver crept down my spine when I passed a particularly gruesome prisoner with spikes protruding from every inch of his skin like some kind of supernatural version of Pinhead from that old horror movie, Hellraiser. I could just imagine the damage he could do to me if he was free.

One more section passed safely, and then my luck ran out. The cell doors were open, and the prisoners were moving about the hallways freely. I heard the whispers as I passed out the trays of food, and a bead of sweat trickled down my face as I tried to push back the fear churning inside of me.

I rushed through the food delivery, practically throwing the food into the cells so I could get out of there as fast as possible. The guard I'd been with had mysteriously "disappeared" so there was no one to help me with what I knew was coming. I winced when some of what was supposed to be mac and cheese splattered across the floor of one of the cells.

Keep it cool, I murmured to myself.

A monster was waiting in the second to last cell. While technically most of the prisoners in this place could be considered a monster, the vampire standing in the doorway of his cell was one of the scariest creatures in the place to me.

It was Julian's second in command, Guthrie. And he looked like he was waiting for me.

"Long time no see, Selena," he purred, somehow still managing to look perfect despite the fact he was in prison too. Evidently, he'd been finding plenty of blood based on his healthy complexion.

"What are you doing in here?" I asked, trying to hide

the tremor in my hands as I passed him a plate of congealed bloody meat that he eyed distastefully. When his gaze flipped from the food back to my face, I knew I'd asked the wrong question. If looks could kill, I'd be six feet under with the scalding hatred he was directing my way.

"Apparently suggesting Julian find another slut to obsess over was the wrong thing to say," he hissed as he took a slight step forward.

I shrugged helplessly and started to push the cart forward. "Sorry about that," I called over my shoulder, the words dying in my throat as his hand shot forward and tightened around my arm.

"What is it about your pussy that has a creature like Julian frothing at the mouth?" A snake-like tongue that I'd definitely not seen before slithered up my neck. I shuddered and tried to pull away, but he held tight.

"I think I'll kill two birds with one stone, little siren. Get a taste of that golden pussy and then collect the bounty from the Warden. I bet your blood will taste good too, even without your power."

I began to thrash around, trying to break free as panic shot through my veins. I didn't want to die, but dying at the hands of a vampire... that was never going to happen.

My frantic attempt to escape was no match for his superior strength, and he dragged me back into his cell with no issue. He threw me down on his cot and straddled my hips, forcing my hands above my head as I continued to jerk around uselessly.

He laughed cruelly and scraped his sharp incisor teeth down my throat. I stiffened in horror, the idea of him biting me, freezing me in place. My breath came out in loud rasps as I started to hyperventilate. His teeth had just pricked my skin and then he was gone, ripped off of me, and the sharp smell of brimstone assaulted my senses.

A harsh tearing sound filled the small cell and I sat up with a gasp, scooting against the wall as I tried to figure out what was happening. I squeaked at what I saw. Black, acrid smoke was seeping out of a wolf-like creature that was currently mutilating and ripping Guthrie's body into a million bloody chunks.

Black spots danced across my vision as my panic increased, but I forced myself to take deeper breaths. The last thing I needed was to pass out, although maybe that would be helpful if I was about to die.

The creature growled as it dropped what looked like Guthrie's leg from its mouth, and then spun around to face me. It took me a second, but a hiccupped sob erupted from my mouth as soon as I realized that the creature in front of me was a hellhound.

"Laaaz?" I squeaked hopefully. I was so screwed if it wasn't. The hellhound shook out its sharp fur and then slowly shifted until Laz was indeed standing in front of me. His eyes glowed red for a second longer before they finally reverted to normal. Without another thought, I threw myself at him, relief clawing at my chest.

"Thank you. Thank you," I whispered fervently into his smooth skin, the faint hint of brimstone suddenly the best smell I'd ever experienced.

His arms came around me and he gripped me tightly. His body was trembling and I noticed that his breathing was labored. "You could have been killed," he whispered gruffly, his shaking increased as he said the words.

It took me a minute, but I realized that this was the opportunity I'd been waiting for.

"The Warden... he's put a bounty on my head. Everyone's trying to kill me," I blurted out, pulling him closer to me.

"What?" Laz roared, his arms squeezing me so tight that I had trouble breathing. His gaze darted across my features like he was afraid that I was going to disappear...or killed at any moment.

"I kind of lost my temper in a meeting with him, and he wasn't happy about it. And ever since then, I've been hunted, chased, and attacked…it's constant. He somehow got the word out to the whole prison."

"Word didn't get to me," he growled darkly. "And it didn't get to the others either. How convenient."

Laz gazed suspiciously out into the hallway, as if someone was going to attack at my moment, which I guess wasn't that far-fetched with how things were going.

It was amazing at how safe I felt at the moment though, like now that I'd been able to tell Laz what was going on, a huge burden had been lifted from my shoulders.

"There was another close call the other day. A raven shifter, or something like that. It was... terrifying," I whispered against his chest, and a deep growl rattled from Laz.

"Let's get out of here," he said urgently before picking me up in his arms and striding out of the cell. I felt the gaze of all the prisoners that we passed, but they stayed away. I'm sure that the bloodied chunks of Guthrie were quite the deterrent. There was no way I wouldn't be forgetting the sight any time soon.

Thinking of it would probably allow me to actually get some sleep tonight. I was obviously fucked up.

Laz turned down an assortment of tunnels. He didn't speak a single word, instead, he remained watchful and alert. Anyone we passed that even seemed to take a step towards us was met with a warning growl that had at least half of them peeing themselves.

It made me feel a little bit better.

"Keon," Laz suddenly barked. And there my love was.

I struggled out of Laz's arms and rushed towards a confused-looking Keon, throwing myself at him like he'd just come home from war. Once again, sobs burst out of me.

"Baby, what's wrong?" he asked softly, stroking my hair with a gentleness that would never cease to surprise and amaze me he was capable of.

"The warden put a fucking bounty on her head," Laz all but roared before I could get a word out.

Similar to Laz's reaction, Keon's entire body stiffened. "What did you just say?"

Laz and I explained the details of what had been happening. Keon was holding me so tightly that it was hard to breathe. As with Laz's reaction, I didn't mind.

"How did all of this happen between when we got back yesterday and today?" Keon asked.

I looked up at him, confused. "Keon, what are you talking about. It's been over a week since we got back from my mother's funeral."

"A week?" he said quizzically. "That's impossible. Selena, no. We just got back." There was an edge of panic threaded through his voice.

"Keon," I breathed. "Why can't you remember?"

Keon's silence was terrifying.

"Lazarus, take Selena back to her cell and don't leave her side. I don't care if fifty guards come to rip you away," he said sternly.

Lazarus nodded his head, a look in his eyes that said he'd like to see them try.

"Keon-" I pressed, but he interrupted me.

"Someone stole the last week from me, Selena. They prevented me from protecting you, from being with you. That's not fucking okay."

"Don't do anything stupid," I pleaded with him.

He shook his head in response.

"Just trust me and go with Laz. I'll find you later, alright?"

I hesitantly nodded my head before letting Laz take my hand and walked away.

I threw a glance over my shoulder before we turned the corner, but Keon was already striding away. I just hoped that whatever he had in mind didn't get him killed.

One thing was clear though, the Warden had definitely found out about us.

* * *

Keon

IT TOOK everything to control myself when my emotions were heightened like this. As I stalked through the halls of the prison, the desire to kill and destroy thrummed through my veins. I'd always been a bit indifferent about the Warden, I was ashamed to admit. I recognized him for the evil, selfish creature that he was, and I gave him a wide berth... or as much of a wide berth as I could while working for him. And though I'd recognized the power he held, I foolishly thought he'd never aim it at me. I'd been living in denial, thinking I could find a way to get Selena out of here without dealing with him. But I thought I at least had time to figure out a plan.

However, that time had obviously expired.

The fact that he'd somehow found a way for me to forget an entire week had my skin crawling. Had he done something in the past like that to me? Were there other pieces of my life that were just gone now?

And he'd done it to make sure that Selena would have to suffer alone. I would have marched to the Warden's office and killed him for that right then if I wasn't sure he would win. The Warden couldn't be beaten physically, but there had to be a way to outsmart him. Or maybe to bargain with him...

"Alaric," I barked as soon as I got to his cell. I unlocked the door and threw it open, a loud clanging echoing down the hallway. "We have a problem."

Alaric had been lounging on his bed, reading a book, but he sat up immediately, his entire body on high alert. You couldn't miss that Alaric was a predator. While I could hide who I was, and did so often, Alaric wore his power proudly.

"What's going on?" he barked.

Recounting what I'd just been told, it didn't take long to realize that Alaric had experienced the same memory loss that I'd experienced.

Alaric let out a loud bellow that threatened to burst my eardrums. I could smell the fear of the prisoners in the air, thick and tangy, like they were sure Alaric was about to come after all of them.

"Where is she?" he asked frantically, striding towards the door. I pulled on his shoulder and narrowly avoided his fist as he tried to come at me for stopping him.

"Laz is with her. She'll be fine. We need to figure out how we're going to get her out of this mess. If Lazarus hadn't been there this time, she would have been dead. What happens when it happens again and someone's not there?"

"He can't be beaten," Alaric said with a sigh as he put his fists down. There was a long silence as he stood there. I could almost see the cogs in his brain working as he thought through the problem. Alaric was a genius. You didn't control one of the world's largest criminal syndicates without being smart.

"I'll go to the Warden. There's got to be something he wants," Alaric finally said, a determined look on his face.

The idea was much less simple than it seemed. A favor from the Warden never came without a price, and after what Selena had done to his treasures… it would be even harder to make him see reason.

"It's going to cost us," I told him, stating the obvious.

"She's worth it," he said fervently.

"She is," I agreed. And she was.

Alaric pushed past me without another word. I followed him out and then headed towards my room to prepare. Although I didn't know what I was preparing for, the goal was clear.

Get Selena out of here. Alive.

CHAPTER 6

ALARIC

My entire life I'd dealt with chaos, and I liked to call it my specialty. But it was a very different thing when it was happening to someone I cared for instead of me. That shit ate me up and spat me out, destroyed. The truth was, Selena's time in Nightmare Penitentiary was always going to be short-lived. Someone as pure and innocent as her didn't belong in a prison, and whether it was her sanity or the lunatics locked up in here, that would get to her first; I knew it was only a matter of time if she remained.

I approached the Warden's door, the guard standing nearby nodding for me to proceed. He understood there was an arrangement between the Warden and me. One where neither of us trusted each other, though we acted like we did. Mutual respect between two enemies.

Raising my arm, I knocked on the door hard.

"Come in," he called from inside his office, and I pushed down the handle and entered. The man... if one could call him that, had his head twisted in my direction while stretching his arm up to place a tiny trinket box up on the top shelf of an empty bookshelf. I'd never once seen his trinkets removed from their display, so this was new. In a corner were several cardboard boxes and in one I noticed some of his artifacts, broken. Now that sight made me smirk like a mad man to see his little toys smashed up. I would have loved to be a fly on the wall when that happened to see his reaction.

"Are you redecorating?" I asked sarcastically.

He growled under his breath. "What do you want, Alaric?"

I shut the door with a click and made my way across the office to his desk. "I have a favor to ask of you."

The Warden turned back around to face me, studying me from behind hooded eyes. The wheels were spinning behind his gaze with how this could possibly benefit him. The guy was so fucking predictable.

"And what would that be?" he asked, sauntering over to the desk, dressed in black tailored pants and a matching button-up shirt. It almost concealed the faint wisp of black mist that came off him today. I had no fucking idea what he was, but now and then snippets of his real self came through. Basically, no one knows shit about him.

He sat in his leather seat, his short hair slick and off his face, and he crossed one leg over the other. Leaning back into his chair, he clasped the armrests. "Go on, I'm listening."

There was a quirk at the corner of his mouth like he'd recently received good news and he fought the urge to let himself smile. Maybe it had been whatever trinket he's just added to this shelf, or maybe it had something to do with my sweet Selena.

I tensed, but refused to let him pick up on my unease. "You and I both have a vested interest in Selena's wellbeing."

"We do?" he said, playing coy, that time his grin splitting his mouth and revealing a perfect line of white teeth.

"I'm not a fool and neither are you, so don't patronize me," I answered.

The shadows around him danced and darkened, as did his expression. "I don't have time for your fuckery. Get out of my face," he barked.

I pressed my back into my seat and stretched my legs out, crossed at the ankles. "Good, now you're ready to listen."

He bristled, and I held back my laughter at how much he loathed not having the upper hand.

"You know as well as me that you wouldn't want Selena to die while under your care. What would the Master Vampire think of that?"

His eyes narrowed, and now we were on the same page. Keon had told us everything that happened at the funeral, along with who we were dealing with.

"And, your point?"

"Look, since she just arrived back from her mother's funeral, she's been attacked several times by inmates ready to kill her. And one was because of a fucking incompetent asshole guard under your command."

He didn't move or say a word.

"So, you want me to punish him? Is that what this is about? Have you forgotten how to take care of your own shit?" His voice hardened, nostrils flaring.

"No, what I want is for you to call off the bounty you placed on her head."

I watched the nerve in his temple twitch.

"And what's in it for me?"

"You get to live another miserable day in this crappy shithole," I answered.

"Is that a threat?" he hissed. The darkness pulsing around him, billowing outward into a hulking outline.

"Not from me, but from the vampire prick who'll come for revenge on you for letting others touch what's his. You know he put her in here for you to just babysit her, right?" From everything I'd learned from Selena and the other guys, her time in Nightmare Penitentiary was her punishment until she submitted to that fucking son-of-a-bitch.

The mists and darkness swirled around him, and he leaned forward in his seat, his elbows on the desk, arms folded over one another. "How about this... I'll offer you a counter deal."

The sneer in his voice was not surprising. Of course, he'd want this to benefit him, he didn't care about Selena. I didn't answer, which gave him the opening to keep going.

"Find me the Cintamani Stone and I will remove the bounty."

I stared at him as his shadows ebbed and then dissolved back into him. "Never heard of it, and you know I can't leave the prison to search for this thing you want?" I swore to Hell, anytime this bastard was given any chance to make a deal, he never wasted the moment. He used others to do his dirty work, to gather more fucking crap to collect dust on his shelves.

"That's the beauty of it," he said, his voice brimming with excitement. "The stone's in the prison."

"What's stopped you from finding it?"

"You think I haven't tried?" He sighed, and he stared over to the shelves behind him. "With the stone, my collection would be close to completion. It's one of a kind, said to have once belonged to Buddha. I've been searching for it my entire life, and when I eventually tracked it down to somewhere inside this prison, I had no choice but to get a job here. It's one of the many reasons I started with Nightmare Corporation."

"You're setting me up to fail," I stated the obvious, and we both knew it. Was this his new way of saying no to me, making up crap about finding impossible relics for him?

"You're scared?" he asked, one of his eyebrows quirking.

"Fuck no, I'm not scared. But I'm a realist. You've been here for what? An eternity and still haven't found it, and now you want me to track down for you a goddamn stone? I need you to remove the bounty from Selena now, not after I complete an impossible mission."

He was on his feet and marching over to his filing cabinet by the wall. With a few punches into the keypad, the lock clicked open, and he started rummaging through the files.

I clenched my hands, suppressing the shudder that flared through me. The anger that demanded I shove his fucking head into the filling cabinet and ram it shut a dozen times at least.

The revelation that he'd asked for something in exchange wasn't new, but what he demanded was ridiculous. He wanted me to go play, find the needle in the goddamn haystack while Selena remained at the mercy of other inmates. The guys and I couldn't be with her every second of the day, as much as I wish I could. I'd get the guards under my control to keep an eye on her. But in truth, there was no guarantee of who the Warden would send on her shifts to deliver food.

"Found it," the Warden called out, like that should somehow make me happy. I growled under my breath in response.

Making his way back to the desk, he hurriedly sat and opened a folder with one sheet of paper in it. And even that only had a paragraph handwritten on it... if that. Was he fucking joking?

"These are my clues," he said.

As much as I fumed, I was fucked. The Warden was an asshole and would toss me out the moment I said no to his stupid request. "Let's hear them."

He clasped the paper with two hands. "There are two items to collect. They are connected and once all merged, they will lead you to the Cintamani Stone. All you need to do is bring me the two objects as I know how to connect them." He looked up at me, the corners of his eyes wrinkling from his excited grin. I contemplated throwing my fist in his face, so he'd stop staring at me that way. "The first is a key, and from what I've discovered so far, it's with one of the guards. They most likely don't even know they have it on them."

"Why the hell is the stone in the prison anyway?"

"Maybe whoever stole the stone went and hid it in the darkest place, where even Buddha couldn't track it down."

I shrugged. Not that I could argue with that since it made sense I supposed. "Okay, so there's a key with a guard?"

"I've searched all the guards, trust me, but nothing.

Either the guard knows or someone else in the prison does and is concealing it. The second object—"

"Wait, wait," I said. "That's all you have? A key that is with a guard?"

"It's no ordinary object and well, I'm guessing it might be concealing itself."

I rolled my eyes. This had to be the worst mission in the world.

"The next item is a scroll case, which I assume holds a map or spell to find the stone. And that's all I have." He lowered the paper back to the folder and closed it. "Bring me both items and you have a deal."

He stared at me like what he'd just told me was the easiest thing in the world.

"For fuck's sake," I muttered. "Now I know why you never found it and why we'll never find it, either. This is a joke. Give me something else to do."

His eyes flashed with anger, then he got to his feet with his thin folder and returned to the filing cabinet. "Take it or get out of my office."

I gritted my teeth, and bitterness rose to the back of my throat. But I didn't move.

"Do we have a deal?" he asked, turning back to face me, standing tall and formidable.

I stared at him with a gaze fueled with hate. Heavy breaths filled the space between us. My mind went over everything he'd told me, over how ridiculous his task was, but it all came down to Selena and her safety and the reminder that she remained an easy target.

"What's so special about the stone?" I asked.

He glanced back to his shelves of collectibles, filling up

the rest of his huge office. "It once belonged to Buddha," he informed me. "Isn't that reason enough?"

I studied him intensely, well aware that things weren't adding up. The stone was one of the reasons he ended up working in the prison, and he'd been searching for it ever since... forever, then he mentioned it would complete his collection. Nope... no way in fucking hell was the Cintamani Stone just a dust collector. There was more to this thing, and he had no plans on letting me know. Which was fine... I'd do my own research.

When I didn't respond, he said, "How about I sweeten the deal. You find me the items that lead to the stone, and not only will I call the bounty off Selena, but I won't give her back to Julian."

"How will you do that?"

"You seem to be under the illusion that I fear the vampire. That's where you're very wrong."

We looked at each other, no words, and we both knew I had no other option but to agree to this insane plan. But considering he'd just added complete protection from Julian for Selena as payment, well, I was suddenly extremely vested in finding the Cintamani Stone.

"Deal." I nodded.

"Good. Now get the fuck out of my face." He smiled widely, the look sickening me.

Before I said something I'd regret, I marched out of his office, and made a beeline straight for the library. I knew the librarian guard, and she'd get me access into the private selection only a few select were permitted. Predominantly the Warden's private collection.

In less than an hour, I was sitting up in the caged section

of the library at the single table with a flickering light overhead, my eyes glued to the ancient book in front of me. The writing was tiny, and I hunched forward to read the only paragraphs I'd found on the Cintamani Stone in these books. It droned on about the stone being special as it had been one of four blessed relics that had fallen from the sky and how it was thought to be one of several Mani Jewels in Buddha's collection, but that no one had ever seen it, so many believe it was a myth. I cursed the Warden internally because if this turned out to be nothing by an illustration of his fucking greedy need, I was going to shove a whole fucking pile of stones down his throat until he choked on them.

I kept reading until I came across a passage that had me catching my breath.

He who possesses the Cintamani Stone, the ancient jewel revered by Buddha, will be granted the extraordinary power of wish fulfilment.

I exhaled loudly and reclined back in my seat. "That damn rat bastard," I murmured under my breath. Of course the Warden wouldn't tell me that part. So what if *we* did find the stone and used it to get her out of prison for good?

My stomach tightened at the thought of how impossible this task was, but we didn't exactly have many other options either.

I shot to my feet and darted out of the library, running through the hallways, searching for Keon and Laz, even Seth would do. I had to tell them what I'd uncovered and that maybe there was a chance to save Selena. I might be deluding myself, but I also refused to give up.

When I searched everywhere and couldn't find any of them, including Seth, who hadn't been in his cell, I found myself swinging back toward Selena's cell. My heart hammered heavily against my rib cage at the possibility of freeing my siren. To be with her outside this hellhole, to adore her like she deserved, to never leave her side.

I slowed when I reached her cell and strolled right inside.

Selena sat curled up on the bed and crying into her hands. My heart shattered like glass at hearing her agony.

"Selena." I moved to her side and sat on the bed with her, taking her into my arms. "Did something else happen? Where the fuck is Laz?"

CHAPTER 7

SELENA

*A*laric was terrifying as he stared around the room, looking like he was ready to murder someone. I ignored his death glare and threw myself at him. It felt like forever since I'd seen him, and I needed to know he was real. Ten guards had dragged Laz away an hour ago. He'd fought back as hard as he could, but eventually, I'd screamed and pleaded for him to stop fighting. I couldn't take watching him get beaten. They'd pulled him away, a look of utter rage and disappointment in himself written across his face. The near-death experience with Guthrie had already left me shaken up. But having Laz taken away like that just reminded me how fucking powerless I was in this place.

If I ever got my power back...

I shivered and wondered for the first time if I even deserved my power back at this point. There was something dark inside of me, something slithering around insidiously, transforming my insides as it went along.

"I knew we couldn't trust that worthless sack of shit,"

Alaric growled, slapping the door shut, and I realized that I'd been so lost in my thoughts that I hadn't bothered to tell him why Laz wasn't here. Crap! The guys weren't exactly thrilled about Laz's sudden place in my life. They were looking for any excuse to push him permanently away at this point.

"He got taken away. Someone must have been watching, and they sent at least ten guards. Laz would have had to slaughter them all to stay and that wouldn't have gotten us anywhere," I told him soothingly. Somehow, his anger was making me calm down. At least calm down enough to stop practically hyperventilating.

"He should have done anything to stay and protect you," Alaric argued, even though we both knew he was just blowing smoke at this point. Alaric pulled me tighter against him, and I soaked in his delicious smell. I wasn't sure how it was possible to smell godlike in a cesspit like this, but somehow Alaric managed it.

"I'm so sorry I wasn't there for you," he groaned into my hair. "I'd die if something happened to you. Right after I burned the whole world down." He pulled away from me and slid one hand around my neck while the other hand slid up to grip my hair. His thumb softly rubbed across my pulse, as if he was reassuring himself that I was still alive. "You were alone this week," he growled, his thumb becoming frantic as I moved.

I couldn't muster up the energy to put on a brave face. It hadn't been his fault. It had been no one's fault but the Warden's. But this week had been one of the hardest of my life. And that was saying something.

"You're here now," I finally stated, staring up at him, suddenly understanding how you could drown in someone's eyes. Caught in the pools of gray, I'm lost in their depths, the color somehow managing to set me on fire and calm me at the same time. I needed to stay in this moment. I needed to forget about everything outside the small walls of my cell. Just for a second.

"You're here now," I repeated softly, his eyes blazing as my hands trailed up his chest. "Now what are you going to do about that?"

He finally got my meaning, and his breath hitched as he licked his lips slowly. He stopped his maddening tracing of my pulse and instead took my face in his hands and kissed me lightly. Impatient, I deepened the kiss immediately; my tongue came out, ready to dance with his. I swallowed his groan as he willingly stepped off the ledge with me, allowing me to desperately pull his shirt off. I dragged my lips away from his and moved them to his chest. His skin was hot to my touch, almost feverish. I licked at the edges of his sharply defined tattoos and let my lips travel along the hard contours of his muscles as he leaned his head back, breathing hard.

He seized me suddenly, taking back control. One arm circled my waist and pulled me close while the other traveled up my back and higher, winding into my hair and forcing my mouth against his. His tongue relentlessly explored my mouth. I loved the way Alaric kissed me. He kissed me like he was starving, and I was the only thing that could satisfy him. His kiss was raw and intense, ripping me open and tangling himself with my insides until I felt like I couldn't live without him.

He leaned me back on the cot. Hovering over me, he used his knee to push my legs apart and I felt the whole thick length of him pushing against my throbbing center.

I stared at him in awe, my gaze heavy-lidded with lust. He was so fucking gorgeous. Broad-shouldered, tanned, and muscular, with a classically chiseled face that was created to destroy hearts. It really wasn't fair for one male to have so much. His tattoos coated his skin, leaving no doubt he was dangerous.

He was also huge, rigid, and erect. Seriously unfair.

My insides convulsed with the desire to feel him.

Alaric slowly undressed me, the movements at odds with the ferociousness of his kiss. He moved me around as if I weighed nothing, somehow not breaking our kiss for a second.

He eased my shirt and bra off with barely a break of our lips. My pants and underwear followed, and then he finally pulled away from me. To look at me. "Fuck, you're perfect," he murmured, his eyes tracing my skin even though he'd seen me naked for what feels like a million times before.

Running his hands down my thighs, he lightly grazed the throbbing place between my legs which was wet and ready. "It fucking kills me to be away from you for a moment. I just want to live in this perfect pussy." I arched underneath him, wanting more and wanting it now.

His dirty words had their own kind of raw power.

It was safe to say that I was obsessed with everything that his mouth did.

I whimpered as he continued to lightly trace my folds, intentionally not giving me what I was desperate for.

Fuck savoring the moment. He needed to give me what I wanted. Now.

With a suddenness that left me breathless, he spread my legs wide. And when I felt the tip of his cock opening me up, I cried out a little from the insane pleasure it brought.

"You make me crazy," he swore and then rammed himself inside of me without warning. Thank fuck he was done holding himself back.

It was impossible to forget how big Alaric was, but my breath still hitched as my body stretched to take him all in. I pulled my knees back, widening my legs as far as they would go, while Alaric withdrew a little and then thrust the whole of his powerful cock in mercilessly. The exquisite mix of pain and pleasure was exactly what I wanted… exactly what I needed.

I urged him to go harder, not caring that my moans were probably carrying throughout the prison hallways. It was reckless, wild, just like Alaric himself. There were no rules right now. Our only focus was chasing pleasure, however we could get it. I lived for this feeling of wild abandon. I never wanted it to end.

I closed my eyes, raising my hands above my head and then gasping when he gripped my wrists hard on either side and used that leverage to increase his rhythm.

"Alaric," I whimpered, "I'm close. I'm so close."

He nipped at my neck. "I know you're close, baby. Fuck. Never. Felt. Anything. As good as you. You're strangling my cock, sweet girl."

I focused every bit of my concentration on the rising wave inside me. I knew what was coming wasn't going to be some quick high that lasted a few seconds and then disappeared. No, Alaric was bringing me somewhere that would consume and shatter me like he did every single time.

He didn't let up as I shook underneath him, that

chaotic ecstasy rising rapidly inside of me with every thrust of his hips against mine. I moaned and shouted, calling out things that would embarrass me if I were able to think at all.

But that was what was perfect about this. I couldn't think at all. All I could do was feel. Pumping into me deep and hard, he waited until I'd gone over the edge before he lost himself in his own ending. I pulled his large hands over my breasts and he kneaded the flesh as he came, shuddering and pushing himself even deeper. I wrapped my legs around him tightly, wanting to keep him inside of me as long as possible while he growled and cursed, filling me with his release.

"Perfect, baby. You're perfect," he whispered as his thrusts slowed down.

The afterglow was real. I swore there were sparkles in the air surrounding us, a haze of glitter that cocooned us on my tiny bed that was barely big enough for one person, let alone two. I sighed, a deep exhale of contentment that was hard to comprehend in a place like this with would-be murderers lurking around every corner. Here in our tiny piece of heaven none of that seemed real. There was only this. Only us.

"Sleep, baby. I'm not going anywhere," he whispered gruffly against my skin as he pulled out with a low groan and curled my body around his.

His order wasn't necessary, though. I was already on my way to dreamland before he was halfway through speaking.

* * *

THE LOW MURMUR of voices woke me up. I blearily opened my eyes and sat up, gripping my blanket tightly so that it still covered me as I looked at who was talking near my cell.

My eyes flew open when I saw Keon and Alaric in a deep discussion, their stoic faces and stiff bodies letting me know they weren't exchanging pleasantries.

"What's happened now?" I asked, my voice coming out gravely from sleep and screaming during sex.

Their gazes flicked to me in tandem, and something fluttered deep in my chest at having both of their attention on me at the same time. I shifted in the bed, feeling ridiculously horny despite the scary vibes I was getting from them. I was about to hear shitty news.

"It's good news," Keon said lightly, his forced cheerful tone ridiculous sounding. The men in my life weren't really "light" individuals. They lived in the dark and I'd fallen in love with them there. Instead of dragging them into the light towards me, I'd willingly followed them into the shadows.

And I think I was alright with that.

"Keon," I groaned, heaving myself off the cot and ignoring their hungry looks as I scrambled into my clothes.

"Seth will be walked to his weekly meeting with the psycho psychologist in ten minutes," Keon said, glancing at his watch. "We need to speak with him."

"Can someone tell me what's going on?" I squeaked as Alaric grabbed my hand the second I'd pulled on my shoes and tugged me out the cell door that Keon had already passed through.

We strode quickly through the halls. Prisoners went

quiet at the sight of Alaric and Keon, and it was nice to walk without feeling like someone was going to jump me at any minute. Several guards passed us. If they thought it was strange that Keon was walking with Alaric and me, they didn't say.

My heart leapt when we turned a corner. And Seth was there, being roughly dragged by an ugly S.O.B. guard who had him by the hair. I opened my mouth to yell at the guard, even though I knew that would be a stupid move, but Alaric squeezed my hand before the words could leave my mouth.

"You're needed in the shifters section," Keon said casually, the authority in his voice leaving no room to argue. The guard leered at me, yanking sharply on Seth's hair once more before releasing it. He was an ugly fucker. Several of his teeth were missing, and there was a jagged white scar stretched across his craggy skin. There was a second of tension where the guard stared at Keon, but finally he shrugged, giving Keon an insincere smile.

"Of course," he said as he walked by us. "You seem to get all the fun assignments, Keon," he called over his shoulder before he disappeared around the corner.

"Selena," Seth called out breathlessly as he stumbled towards me. It looked like he'd gone through another beating recently. There were dark bruises marring his beautiful skin. Keon undid his cuffs, and he was on me before I could examine him further. He buried his face in my neck, almost pushing me to the ground as he did so. It was only Alaric's hands on my back that kept me up. Seth took deep inhales, and I cringed thinking I probably smelled like dirty sex and the prison. Seth didn't seem to mind, though. He cuddled against me, continuing to breathe me in, like I was covered in strawberries and cream instead of sweat and cum.

"Seth," I whispered, stroking his hair softly and thinking how good it felt to feel him against me. Seth was complicated. A hard, beautiful shell surrounded the most perfect heart I'd ever seen, and the moments where he gave me a glimpse of it were worth everything. It killed me what he was forced to go through in this place.

"Dale will be back soon. Fucker knew I was lying," Keon stated, shifting uncomfortably at Seth's overt display of affection.

"Just one more minute," Seth murmured, his lips tracing my skin and sending shivers down my spine. He slid his hands into my hair and tilted my head back for better access. My stomach dropped as our mouths met and our tongues collided, a throbbing starting between my legs. The kiss wasn't sweet or sensual. It was desperate, like every moment seemed to be with him since I'd met him.

Fisting his jumpsuit, I pulled his body to mine. His cock pressed into my stomach, making my knees weak. My brain stopped functioning, my body controlling its need. His hips pushed further, his thickness growing against me as I arched back. A small part of my brain realized that he was pushing me against Alaric... who was also growing hard.

"Seth," Alaric grumbled, trying to sound annoyed, but it was obvious he was affected by what was going on.

"Fuck," Seth growled, bringing his forehead to mine; his breathing as erratic as mine. "There's never enough time."

Alaric pulled me away from Seth, and my brain started functioning again.

"I made a deal with the Warden," Alaric abruptly announced.

And that announcement definitely pushed my brain into hyper-drive.

"What kind of deal?" Seth asked sharply.

"We're getting Selena out of here," Keon answered.

"But how?" I asked, a stupid pulse of hope beating in my chest.

"The Warden loves his treasure. So, I made a deal for Selena's release… in exchange for a little treasure hunt."

"That sounds easy," Seth said sarcastically. He'd taken my hand and was gripping it tightly, his hand slightly trembling in mine.

"What kind of treasure hunt?" I prodded.

"There's a stone somewhere in this place. Or at least there's supposed to be. One that's supposed to grant wishes," answered Alaric.

"Like that ridiculous Aladdin's lamp that humans are so fond of hearing about?" Seth scoffed.

I glanced at Seth, wondering why his attitude seemed to get worse.

"So, that's really it, we just go on this treasure hunt...and then we're out?" I pressed, the seed of hope growing bigger.

Alaric's face dimmed. "We're still figuring out the 'we' part," he admitted.

Before I could say anything else in response, the sound of boots marching towards us echoed down the hallway.

"Shit. That's Dale. We need to move," Keon hissed.

We dashed down the hallway, away from the footsteps that were rapidly approaching.

"So what's the plan?" asked Seth when we stopped. "Where do you start a search for this magic stone?"

Alaric nodded towards Keon. "He's up first. Keon, you know the guards. One of them has the key."

Keon nodded like he perfectly understood what Alaric was saying, telling me they'd spoken about the treasure hunt earlier.

Seth and I just exchanged confused looks.

"Keon," Dale suddenly hissed, appearing through a doorway in the stone wall that I could have sworn wasn't there a second ago. "No one in the shifter section seemed to know why I would have been called there," he said, suspicion and dislike written all over his face.

"My bad," Keon said calmly. "I guess you can finish your task." I gave Seth a panicked look, realizing he was about to be taken from me once again.

Dale muttered under his breath as he tugged on Seth and pulled him away. Somehow Keon had slipped the handcuffs back on and my heart lurched at the sight of Seth walking away, the picture of dejection.

Keon nodded at me before striding after Seth.

"Treasure hunting, huh?" I finally said, as I watched them leave.

"Always was a big fan of Treasure Island," Alaric replied lightly as I rolled my eyes.

I wouldn't get my hopes up. That never worked well for me.

Or at least that's what I told myself...

CHAPTER 8

SELENA

I buttoned up my orange jumpsuit, ready for breakfast, but I hadn't left yet. Trepidation had me too scared to go out on my own. I had no clue who would or wouldn't be waiting to attack me. It freaked me out to think that I was so paranoid now.

"Head's up," a female's voice called from behind me.

I snapped around just as an orange candy bar was flying right at my face. Instinct had me snatching it right out of the air, my pulse racing at how quickly I did that. I looked at the package of Reese's peanut butter cups in my hand, then up at Nova, who stood in the doorway.

"Hey girl," she said, strolling into my cell, dressed in orange prison pants and a black tee tucked into them. Her short light hair was slick and off her face like she'd just come out of the shower. "Figured I'd pay you a visit and see how you were after the bird douche attacked you the other day."

"You make it sound so casual," I answered with a smile

on my face. "I think that the raven shifter is going to be in my nightmares forever."

She laughed and leaned a shoulder against the wall near my bed. "Trust me, if I had it my way, I would have zapped him out of existence before you got there, but the fuckwit with shriveled balls had a way of sneaking up on people when they least expected it."

I couldn't help but laugh with her. "So, your spell not only decimated him but shriveled his balls?" The moment the words left my mouth, I felt stupid asking such a crazy question while imagining her finding his balls among the pile of black feathers.

"Oh, no girl, I had the horrible experience of seeing them firsthand because he was also a flasher. And they were already dried up prunes. Gag." She faked a gag reflex, which only had me laugh harder, bringing tears to my eyes. "You know that's why he was eating eyes... to help improve his sexual stamina. Fucking lunatic."

"I'm glad you got rid of him," I said, looking at the chocolate bar, my mouth salivating.

"And I owe you my life for being there at the right moment. So, thank you. All I had to give you was that package of Reese's. It's my favorite."

"Want to share?" I said, already tearing the wrapper.

"You know it."

I handed her one of the two treats in the packet, and as she peeled it from the paper and popped it into her mouth, I quickly did the same. The chocolate peanut buttery goodness melted on my tongue, and I moaned at how incredible they tasted. "I've never had these before but I'm in love."

"Right?! Anyway, feel like joining me for breakfast?"

I nodded instantly. I'd seen what she did to the raven shifter, so I felt safer with her in my company.

"Not many people would do what you did with the Raven. No one sticks their neck out for anyone here, so I could tell right away, you're a decent person. And I'll give you one piece of advice. Don't go back down to that cell block on your own ever again. It's filled with sickos."

"Is that where your cell is?" Then, like a hammer to my head, I realized how rude I sounded, implying she was a sicko. "Shit, I didn't mean you were like that. Just that... you know it's a dangerous place, and--"

She patted my arm, offering me a kind smile. "Nope, my cell isn't there, but I was visiting someone and well, that was a mistake I won't be repeating."

Nova seemed nice. She reminded me of myself, where she always expected the worst in people, so when someone did the opposite, it was a pleasant surprise.

"What are you in this joint for?" she asked as we strolled down the hallway toward the mess hall. We fell into the mass of inmates gravitating for their morning meals.

"For not giving my virginity to the asshole master vampire." The thought of Julian left a bitter taste in my mouth, bringing back images of Mom's funeral. My chest tightened, but I didn't want to let it get to me. I'd cried enough at the unfairness of everything. So, I blinked away the tears.

"Fuck! That's twisted and wrong. If I ever get out, I'd gladly destroy him for you."

I grinned at how wonderful that sounded. Having him gone would solve so many of my problems. "What about you?" I asked, to distract myself from thinking of Julian.

"Arsen."

I cut her an incredulous look. "You're in here because you burned something down? Sounds like you got jerked around as much as me."

"Well, to be fair, I burned down three homes, all belonging to an Alpha werewolf who'd enslaved females with every intention of forming a cult and breeding hundreds of pups."

"Eww. What a freak."

"Yep, and they imprison me here while he's still out there. On the bright side, I got my sister out from under his thumb and to safety." She gave me a crazy smile and two thumbs up before schooling her features, and continued talking, which only made me like her even more. Why hadn't I met Nova before?

During breakfast, I barely paid attention to the usual madness of people arguing, or even the brawl over a brownie. Instead, all I could think about was that I actually had a friend like some normal person. She talked about her family, about how she struggled to fit in, how she was homeschooled because most schools that accepted supernaturals were too afraid of someone with powers.

"I think it's amazing you're a wizard. When I think that, of course my mind goes to Harry Potter and that you are super powerful."

She chuckled at me. "Farthest from the truth. My mother is human and my father is a wizard, but he ditched the family when I was a baby. And I wish there was a magic school like Hogwarts... But alas, I was sent to a normal school with humans. For so many years, my mother forced me to hide my abilities. Though to be fair, I never had full control of them in the first place. So, when I accidentally turned the entire class into raccoons, it was homeschooling for me." She smiled and continued to eat her scrambled eggs, but I heard the heartache in her voice.

"Is it sad that I'm happy to have met you and that we both have horror stories to share from growing up?" I said then took a bite of cold toast with no butter because they'd run out in the kitchen.

"Absolutely. Maybe we need a regular girls' session over a meal. When you're not with one of your guys of course."

Her words caught me off guard and I stammered for a response.

"Crap. I went and put my foot in my mouth, didn't I? I didn't mean to sound like a jealous bitch, trust me I'm not. I mean, if I could get just one guy interested in me, I'd be ecstatic. It's just that this place is dead boring and everyone talks about everyone's business, and some of the other women have noticed how lucky you are."

"They're talking about me?" I gasped at the thought.

"Most of them would love to be in your position. What a problem to have… where to put four dicks." She giggled, almost like a schoolgirl. "I'm just saying. I mean… well done, but also, they are some freaking dangerous guys too. I shouldn't ask, but have you had a foursome with them?" She was rambling, and I could see the excitement in her eyes, and I started to think that she might have been one of the women in the prison talking about me, too.

I shook my head. "Things are complicated, to say the least, between me and the four of them."

She was hanging off my every word. "I can just imagine. I once watched a show with a guy with three wives, and half the time, they were just bickering about spending more time with the dude."

I swallowed the food in my mouth. "Well, there have definitely been some scary moments between the guys when I swore they would kill each other."

"My mother once told me to find myself a good human man because all supernaturals were monsters. But you know what I think?" She leaned in closer, like what she was about to tell me was a secret. "I'm all about falling for monsters. They're powerful, dominating, and will protect you against anyone. I swear when I see a huge guy, I act all cavewoman, craving him, imagining how it would be to be fucked by him." She leaned back with a sigh. "I know, I sound crazy, but then again, I haven't been with a guy for over eight months. That does stuff to a person." She grinned lopsidedly.

"The cavewoman thing is true when I'm around my guys." It was strange calling them *my guys,* but in truth, I was sort of with them now. Maybe more because what I felt for them had my heart clenching. I came into this prison feeling alone and terrified, and I ended up losing my heart, totally worth it.

"So, what is the deal with Seth? He's locked up, beaten. I mean, that's got to be hard to be with someone like that."

I wasn't sure how to respond; I hadn't spoken to others about my personal life, but there was also a type of freedom in not holding it all inside, either. At the same time, though, doubts crept through my mind at all her questions, almost crippling me with the fear that Nova was only being nice to me for ulterior motives. But how much of that was me being paranoid? Nearly everyone I'd ever known had used me? I took a deep breath, willing my racing heart to settle down before I had a full-blown panic attack from one question.

"I won't lie, it's hard," I finally said. "It kills me to see him punished so severely." I didn't say too much more, especially after what I'd seen through his crystal about his past. Those were personal moments not meant for anyone else.

I stared down at my half-eaten meal, suddenly missing Seth and already making plans for when I could visit him.

Nova placed her hand on mine, and I lifted my head to meet her dark gaze. "I can help you with Seth?"

"What do you mean?"

"I've seen the state of the brutal beatings he receives, how much agony he's in. I can give you something for him so he feels less pain. It might even give you and him more time to spend together."

I blinked at her. "You can do that?"

"I'm not the strongest or most in control wizard, but I have an affinity to healing. I can make a small batch of something to help him with the pain after the beatings. Would that help, you think?"

"Yes, absolutely," I said, a bit too loud in my excitement. "I mean, that would be an incredible gift for him. Thank you."

"Like I said, you saved me and I owe you."

"I thought the chocolate was the payment," I teased her.

"While I love Reese's Peanut Butter Cups, giving you chocolate does not equate to saving my life."

"Unless, of course, it's a huge crate's worth," I say, then shovel more egg into my mouth, holding back a laugh.

"Is that your way of asking for more?"

I shrugged, wiping my mouth with a napkin. "I would never say no to more. How do you get them here, anyway?"

"The trick to surviving this place is to barter. Everyone has something to offer, so it's all about finding out who has what. This is where my power comes in handy. There's this guard who brings me chocolate in exchange for small love spells he sells outside the prison."

"I wish I would have run into you earlier. Might have made my stay here easier to have someone just to talk to. Most people look at me like I've got two heads, so this is nice."

"When I first arrived, I was beaten so many times, I ended up unconscious every second day. Only after I fought back, did people leave me alone. It's like a fucking wolf pack in here, and to not be walked over, you gotta bite back. But lucky for you, you've got your men to help you too." She grinned and returned to her breakfast.

That uncertain trepidation flashed back again, about how many times she kept mentioning the guys. Except, the way we met was pure coincidence, right? And I wanted, with every fibre in my being, to believe that she was exactly what she appeared to be. A friend.

CHAPTER 9

SELENA

I wheeled my meal cart down the hall hurriedly, throwing a glance behind me every couple of minutes any time I heard what I thought were footsteps. Things had been mercifully quiet, though. Like the Warden was giving us a brief reprieve to hunt down his treasure before finishing me off. There still wasn't a guard with me, though, which in this case was a good thing.

My stomach churned with nerves, wondering what Seth would think of the potion I had in my pocket. The last thing he wanted from me was pity, so anytime he suspected it, he got really upset. But what I was feeling wasn't pity; it was helplessness. And this was one small thing I could do to help him.

A flicker of unease hit me when I wondered if I could trust Nova. I'd obviously tell Seth where I got it and leave it up to him to decide if he wanted it or not... but at least it was something. And if he didn't want the potion, I also had the scepter stowed in the bottom of the meal cart.

Maybe just having a second to reconnect with it would help him.

I turned the corner and there he was, leaning against the wall in his cell where he was sketching in a notebook. He looked up when he heard my cart, his eyes glowing with happiness the second he saw me. There was a fresh cut across his left eyebrow, like he'd been struck and it had split open.

Which was probably what happened.

"Selena," he said, the rare smile on his face turning him from stunning to out of this world beautiful.

"Hi," I whispered, looking around to see if anyone was lurking. When I heard nothing beyond the usual dreadful moans and screams of the prisoners, I dashed to open the cell, using the key Keon had given me to unlock Seth's door. For a second, I imagined taking Seth's hand and just making a run for it.

It was nice to dream, at least.

He dropped what he was working on and pulled me into his arms, and I sighed. When I really thought of it, it was a little scary that I only felt at home when I was in their arms. When did that happen?

Seth groaned when I put my arms around him, and I realized that he once again had lashes on his back. Wild, white-hot rage flooded my body when I thought of the Warden and what he was allowing to happen in this place. I hurriedly pulled away and grabbed the vial of potion from my pocket.

"I got this for you. It's supposed to help you heal faster," I told him before explaining the somewhat suspicious circumstances of where I'd gotten it from.

Seth eyed it dubiously before his shoulders fell and let

out a long sigh. "I'm tired," he admitted. The vulnerability in his eyes silently asked me for my encouragement.

"It doesn't make you weak," I whispered to him.

That seemed to be what he was waiting for because he grabbed the vial, tipped his head back and swallowed without wasting another second.

We waited a moment, and then he gripped his throat frantically and started sputtering and choking.

"Seth!" I screeched, panic and guilt coursing through me.

He paused and winked at me with a snort. "Gotcha," he teased.

I stared at him in disbelief for a minute before I punched him in the shoulder. "Don't do that, you asshole! You scared me."

"But it was sorta funny, right? Besides, I had to break up the mood. I feel like it's always doom and gloom when you're with me because I'm such a morose bastard," he said with a shrug.

I was about to argue with him until I noticed the blush on his cheeks, and his overall color was starting to look better. And I stared in amazement as I watched the cut over his eye heal.

"Seth," I whispered excitedly, already planning how I could get a gallon of that stuff for him.

"I feel amazing," he purred, stretching his arms out above his head. "This is amazing."

I giggled in absolute delight as he picked me up off the ground and spun me around. I'd never seen him so... light.

He set me down, his eyes dancing in a way I wanted to keep forever. "Oh! I have one more thing for you," I told him, remembering the scepter I had stashed in the cart.

I dashed over, grabbed it, and brought it over to Seth. He looked longingly at it for a long moment before he reached out. Right as his fingertips grazed the scepter, the world went black...

* * *

My eyes opened, and I gasped as I stared at my surroundings.

I knew this place...

That obsidian-colored marble floor... the glittering walls. This was the castle I had the vision of the last time I'd touched the scepter.

I really never learned.

Except... a soft gasp caught my attention. I looked to my left and saw Seth there, staring at his surroundings in shock and awe... and a million other emotions that I had trouble deciphering.

He finally noticed I was standing next to him, and his eyebrows shot up in surprise. "How did we...?" His voice trailed off as he glimpsed a balcony off to his left, where I could see a sparkling aquamarine sea in the distance that made Cancun's perfect waters look like a joke.

"It's a vision," I whispered to him as his hand took mine and dragged me towards the balcony.

Something that was half laugh, half sob bursted out of his mouth when we reached the balcony and looked upon what I assumed was Fairie.

I'd never seen anything so... perfect. Everything was brighter here, like the gods had leveled up when they'd created it, giving it the best of everything. The glimpse I had before hadn't been enough to make a tremendous impact. But what I was seeing now... It's the kind of beauty you would yearn for your entire life if you left it and never got to see it again.

I understood more than ever the pain Seth was experiencing at losing this. I was going to be changed after losing this.

Footsteps sounded down the hall and Seth snapped to attention like he'd been in a trance. He grabbed my hand and pulled me behind one of the enormous curtains that buttressed the entrance to the balcony. Voices got louder as they approached.

"The reports show our instructions are being carried out exactly as given. Eventually, he'll do the job for us and just beg for death," one of the voices laughed.

Seth stiffened next to me. "No," he whispered, horror etched across his beautiful features. That's when I realized he was whole here. All evidence of the prison's destruction had disappeared from his face. The only difference between this Seth and the Seth in the first vision I'd seen was the sorrow in his eyes.

A female's voice giggled, and now I was stiffening. Because I recognized the sound of that voice, even just from the laugh.

It was Seth's fiancee or ex-fiancee, I should say.

That bitch.

"What-" I tried to whisper, but Seth put a finger to his lips. The voices quieted as they passed and went further down the hallway. We stood there frozen for what felt like forever before Seth grabbed my hand and pulled me from behind the curtain. Staying close to the wall, he led me down the hallway towards where the two fae had gone. There was a tic in Seth's cheek as we moved quickly, his gaze staying locked on the end of the hallway. He stopped in front of a door and laid his ear against it, which appeared to be made of solid gold before grimacing at whatever he heard.

Seth waved his hand in front of the door and muttered a few words before opening it without a sound. I tried to ask what we were doing, but no sound came out. I realized Seth had somehow silenced everything. He squeezed my hand, and then we walked through the door, our footsteps completely silent.

As we walked into a room fit for a king, a loud grunting filled the air. I looked at Seth in alarm, thinking his spell or whatever he'd done was fading, but he just shook his head. Deciding to trust that Seth would handle it, I followed him around another corner.

And then promptly wanted to pull my eyeballs out and break my eardrums as I realized what the groaning was.

Seth's fiancee was riding the mystery man that I'd seen in my first vision like he was the horse of her dreams. Except I was feeling good about my ability to please Seth after watching this display...because she was terrible at it.

She may have been beautiful, but she was no cowgirl.

Seth didn't seem upset by his ex's erratic thrusting. His gaze was locked on the groaning man underneath her; suspicion and devastation clouded his gaze. I squeezed his hand to get his attention and gave him a questioning look, nodding towards the couple.

"My brother," he mouthed, and I let out a silent gasp. That would explain why the ebony haired fae looked like him. And that meant...

Before I could say anything, Seth's brother let out a loud groan as he finished with gusto. He immediately flipped the girl off him, and I grinned because obviously she hadn't finished. And he stared contentedly at the ceiling, especially pleased with himself.

The girl visibly rearranged her disappointed face and cuddled up next to Seth's brother. "Tell me again how it will happen," she purred, using her finger to trace circles all over his chest. I stared in rapt fascination at the pair of them, the pieces arranging themselves in my mind.

I pulled on Seth's hand, and he glanced over at me. "Your brother killed your father," I mouthed. He didn't look surprised, and I realized that the scene before us must have given him more answers than I could imagine.

"We have spies in the prison spending day and night looking for the scepter. And as soon as we find that... and the crystal, no one will have any doubt that I'm the king. Seth will die, and I will rule this land for eternity." Seth's brother spoke the words dreamily. And I wanted to throw up.

"Why don't we just kill him now?" the bitch asked, her hand sneaking closer to his flaccid cock.

"Because if Seth's figured out the perfect hiding place and they can't find the scepter, then it will be lost forever. There are more secrets in that prison than anywhere else in the world."

"How do you know Seth even has the scepter?" she asked in a baby voice that was worse than nails scratching on a chalkboard.

"I just do," he announced darkly before grabbing her head and forcing it towards his hardening dick.

Seth had heard everything he needed to know. And luckily, he dragged us out of the room before I was traumatized by all the moaning. The spell lasted until we'd made it to what seemed like the other side of the castle. The spell abruptly snapped, the smell of magic sizzling in the air as Seth's heavy breathing filled the silence.

"Seth," I whispered as I watched him break apart in front of me. His elbows fell to his knees as he hunched forward, inhuman noises erupting from his mouth. He abruptly stood up and yelled so loudly I was sure every occupant in the castle... and out of the castle could hear him.

"The person I was closer to than anyone else in the world betrayed me. He stole everything from me," Seth said brokenly, his eyes staring at me unseeingly, like he wasn't speaking to me. "How do you get past that?"

I closed my eyes, feeling his pain in my heart as if it was my own.

* * *

MY EYES FLEW OPEN, and I gasped when I realized we were still standing in Seth's cell, both of us holding the scepter. Compared to the Technicolor dream world we'd just come from, the prison seemed even more dark and depressing.

Seth was just staring at the scepter as if in a daze.

Before I could say anything, pounding footsteps filled the hallway. I really needed to learn Seth's trick if I ever got my power back, and then I would silence all footsteps permanently. They were the harbinger of only bad things.

"It's a guard," Seth snapped in panic. Our gazes both flew to the scepter.

"Hide it," I gasped, stating the obvious. I was a fool to have brought it here... though now Seth knew who had betrayed him.

I'd need to unravel all of that at a later time.

Seth dropped to his knees and dug his nails into the concrete and rocks under his cot. Suddenly, a stone popped up and Seth dropped the scepter into the hole it revealed before quickly covering it right back up and grabbing the notebook he was sketching in. I darted to the cart and grabbed a food tray just as the guard appeared from around the corner. That was another thing I wanted to get rid of, corners. My house needed to just be one long line so no one could be lurking anywhere.

"Get going," the guard barked and I hurriedly pushed my cart away, not wanting to attract any attention.

Once again, I left another piece of my heart in Seth's cell. At this rate, I wasn't going to have any pieces left if I ever did get out of here to actually survive...

* * *

A SOFT CARESS across my face woke me from a fractured sleep filled with memories I didn't want to relive but was forced to courtesy of my dreams.

"Keon?" I asked blearily as I sat up and saw him standing beside my cot.

"Sorry to wake you, princess. We're meeting with the others and have to hurry."

I nodded, still half asleep and hurriedly changed clothes before Keon and I walked out of my cell. We made our way to Alaric's cell, where he and Laz were in a tense discussion. Their gazes snapped to us as we walked inside. Before I could even ask what we were here to discuss, since it had taken me the entire walk to even form complete sentences, the guys started bickering back and forth.

Apparently, the search for the guard wasn't going well.

"I've made it through at least a hundred so far," Keon groaned angrily. "None of them have the key. And I'm beginning to arouse suspicion."

"So, keep going. There have to be rumors about some of the older guards who have been here forever," snapped

Alaric, obviously not feeling sympathetic to Keon's whining.

"If you're so confident it's such an easy job, why don't you do it," Keon hissed.

"Well, we have to give you something to do since you wouldn't be able to contribute anything else," Alaric responded cockily.

The guys continued to snap at each other; it was way too much for me to deal with in the middle of the night.

"Guys," I said wearily as Keon and Alaric fought back and forth. I sighed when they appeared to not hear me.

"I'm taking Selena back to her cell," Laz announced, and that got their attention.

"I can take her," Alaric and Keon snapped almost simultaneously.

"You both seem to have a lot more to talk about and Selena's dead on her feet," Laz said firmly. "I'm taking her."

Both Alaric and Keon looked at me expectantly, like they wanted me to pipe up, that I wanted one of them to take me back to my cell. I was unamused by the macho shit show I'd just witnessed, though, and getting away from them sounded really good actually.

So I kept silent.

Laz smartly held his tongue and didn't gloat as he led me out of Alaric's cell. I could feel Keon and Alaric's shocked and disappointed stares on me all the way down the hall.

"That was fun," I finally said after we'd been walking silently for a while.

Laz made a half-hearted, non-committal sound, and I gazed over to look at him to see what he was thinking. He appeared to be in deep thought.

A dirty coin skittered down the dank hallway as we walked, and I smiled and picked it up. "Penny for your thoughts?" I purred.

He snorted. "Cute, princess," he murmured, but his serious mood didn't lift.

I stopped and gently touched his shoulder. "Seriously Laz, what's wrong?"

"Nothing," he said stiffly, but it was easy to tell he was lying. "Let's just get back to your cell."

We walked in silence the rest of the way. The journey was long enough for my anger to build. Stupid, stupid men. All of them.

"Bye," I told him, turning my back to him in a way that hopefully clearly illustrated I was telling him to fuck off.

Laz sighed deeply but didn't leave.

I swirled around indignantly. "Is there a reason you're still here?" I fumed.

He stared at me, biting at his lip so savagely I was half afraid he was going to tear it off.

"What's up your ass, princess," he sneered.

I balled up my fists angrily. "I don't know what I did wrong. Why are you treating me like this?" The words came out half-sobbed. I was tired, frustrated, and over-whelmed. Basically, a basket case of emotions.

"You haven't asked me to go with you," Laz exploded.

Shocked, I stumbled back a few steps. "What do you mean?"

"Don't be an idiot," he snapped. "I'm entangled into this plan to get you out of here, spending night and day strate-gizing with Alaric and Keon, and you haven't even asked me to go with you once we get you out."

I gaped at him. "Of course, you'll come with me," I

blurted out, the rightness of the words settling deep inside of me. Suddenly, I couldn't imagine a world where Laz didn't come with me. He felt necessary for any chance of happiness.

When did that happen?

"Why haven't you said anything?" Laz replied, vulnerability creeping into his voice.

I thought for a moment, a thousand excuses on the tip of my tongue. "I guess I thought it was obvious," I murmured. And that was the truth. I'd assumed that all of them would be coming with me somehow. Did they not know that?

Laz walked towards me and just stood there, studying my face. "I wish you could see what was right in front of you," he said sadly.

"I don't understand," I murmured, hating that I was the cause of the sadness in his eyes.

"I'm the only one that's just here for you," Laz told me as we stared at each other. "Alaric wants to find the stone and whatever other secrets there are in this place to increase his power and take over the world. The fae wants to get his kingdom back. Keon feels a sense of duty to this place and is a fucking serial killer with an urge to kill everything around him. But me, Selena, I just want to be there for you… to make you happy."

There were a million arguments I could have made in defending my other men's honor. But the words he was saying… They did something to me. Although he was wrong in so many ways, he was also right in other ways about Keon, Seth, and Alaric. And for a girl who'd always been overlooked or used, whose own mother had treated her terribly, his words were a balm to my soul.

"All I want to do is love you," he told me in a throaty whisper, his gaze searching my face for answers. "Please, just let me."

Warmth filled up my insides, threatening to overflow. This beautiful, incredible creature was telling me he was mine.

How did I get so lucky?

"So love me then," I murmured, and I watched as his face erupted in happiness when my words sunk in.

"You don't even have to love me back," he told me, all but begging as his hand caressed my cheek like I was extremely precious.

"You're a terrible negotiator, Lazarus," I scolded softly, my eyes closing in delight as his hand continued to trail all over my skin. "And it's too late to offer me a way out, not when I've already fallen."

Laz's breath hitched at my pronouncement. "Are you saying-"

"Yes, Laz," I told him, getting up on my tippy toes to lay a gentle kiss on his perfect lips.

"I need the words, Selena."

"Lazarus. I love you," I announced.

Before I could say anything else, his lips were on mine, devouring me whole like he was a dying man and I was his last meal. Owning the very breath from my body. His mouth moved against mine as his hands cradled my face. He kept me firmly against him, our lips staying fused. Running the tip of his tongue across the seam of my lips, I moaned, and he pushed his way into my mouth. His kiss forced my feet to move with him as he backed me against the wall. I was trapped between the cool stone of the wall and the heat of Laz's body. It was a delicious feeling.

He leaned back and studied me like a lion about to strike his prey. His gaze flashed. "Say it again," he ordered, and I smiled as his lips hovered a few inches from mine, washing his warm breath over my own.

"I love you," I told him. My pulse raced as he closed in on what looked like pure bliss.

"Thank you," he murmured as his hand grazed my neck, sliding down my shoulder before he ran his fingers across my arm. This time I was the one who grabbed his face in my hands, brought our lips together, and kissed him. It didn't take a second for Laz to take control, sliding his tongue against mine. Both our breaths were heavy as we drank each other in. His kisses were drugging, the kind of hit I wanted to experience every day, over and over.

Laz led me from the wall and pushed me to my cot until I was lying on my back. My heart took off in a gallop as his hands moved from my hips and up my chest as he easily removed my shirt.

"It's hard to comprehend such beauty exists in the world," he declared while his gaze caressed my body. The passion in his eyes was hard to miss, but under that was a layer of love so strong that it felt hard to breathe.

"The way you look at me," I whispered in an aching voice. "It's something to me. Right here," I told him, as my hand rested on my pounding heart.

"Kiss me," I all but begged. He didn't make me wait. His mouth was on mine in an instant. His hand cupped my cheek, providing the tenderness to offset the force of his lips. I tried to pull his shirt off, needing the skin-to-skin contact, but I couldn't remove it. He pulled away from me for a second, stripping off his shirt in one move, the universal sexy guy move that I'm pretty sure I could watch over and over again and never get bored.

My hellhound was a thing of beauty. Sleek lines and tatted skin. I watched as his muscles tensed as I brushed my fingers across his skin, wanting to explore every inch of him.

"What does this one mean?" I asked, gliding to a Latin phrase, *Flectere si nequeo superos, Acheronta movebo*, typed in small subscript letters across his rib cage.

"If I cannot sway the heavens, then I will raise hell," he said throatily, his eyes closing in pleasure as I continued to caress his skin.

My hands glided to his chest. "And the skull in the cage?"

"To remind me that no matter where they put me, I will always be free."

My heart hitched at his blank tone. "That's beautiful," I breathed. "This one?" I brushed along his shoulder, following the shape of the giant enchanted rose that I was pretty sure was from Beauty and the Beast. "Disney's a little different for a hellhound."

"To remind me that happily ever afters can happen… even for a beast." I giggled because it was kinda corny, but also kinda hot that this big, strong, scary hellhound shifter believed in happily-ever-afters.

"You're perfect," I whispered as his lips danced across my skin again.

Laz pulled the straps of my bra off slowly, placing soft kisses on my neck before fully removing it. Our mouths found each other again as his hand moved to my breast. Pulling the nipple between his fingers, rolling it, causing me to moan.

"The sounds you make are so damn sexy," he declared as his mouth moved lower.

"Laz," I gasped his name as he licked around my nipple before taking it into his mouth. My hand went to his hair, fisting it and holding him there as his other hand moved to my pants. Together we worked to get them and my underwear off until I was lying fully naked underneath him. He moved back to my mouth, kissing me hard while he drove me crazy with his hands. I gasped when his finger found my clit and he began to make a circular motion, which sent immediate heat spiraling throughout my body.

"Want this every day," he murmured against my ear. "I want to hear those moans and feel this perfect pussy. I don't want a day to go by without being inside you." His words combined with the way he increased the pressure on my clit and then inserted a finger, were driving me insane. My head lolled back and forth on the bed as pleasure surged through me.

"Please," I begged.

"Please, what?" Laz growled as his teeth dragged against my skin.

I didn't have an answer for him. I'm not even sure what I need at this point. Only that I need more. More of him. More of what he's doing. Just more.

My fingers tangled in his hair while he continued to move his fingers in and out of me while simultaneously keeping up that perfect pressure on my clit. My mouth dropped open as I fell over the edge, plummeting in a fall I never wanted to end.

Laz moaned against my neck while I screamed his name. The self-satisfied smirk on his face only made him hotter. I slid my hands down his chest and quickly removed his pants. I slowly freed his cock, trying not to let on how desperate I was for it. Lazarus flipped over onto his back with ease, obviously knowing where this was headed.

"Fuck," he groaned as I gripped him tightly in both hands. His skin heating, beads of sweat deliciously spread across his skin. I kissed my way down his abdomen, my tongue leaving a trail as I went.

"Are you going to suck my cock, little siren?" he growled. Looking up at his beautiful face, I swore I could see flecks of fire in his gaze.

I moaned in delight as my lips kissed the tip of his cock reverently. His groans filled the cell as I wrapped my lips around his cock, pulling him deep into my mouth as I moved up and down, paying special attention to the underside with my tongue. The noises that fell from his lips are a mix of curses and praise and my cheeks flushed as I felt him watching me avidly.

His noises were so fucking sexy.

"Fuck, sweetheart," he all but shouted as I worked to hollow out my cheeks and force him to the back of my throat. Laz's fingers gripped my hair tightly, pulling on it just enough to give me an edge of pain with my pleasure. I fucking loved it.

He pulled me off him suddenly, our groans melding together in the air. "I'm not coming until I'm inside of your pussy," he growled as I pouted at my fun being stopped. Before I could try to convince him otherwise, he flipped me over so fast that I was dizzy. He threw my legs over his shoulder and then he was feasting on me. That was the only way to describe it. He devoured me, his tongue spearing me over and over, while his perfect fingers paid attention to my clit. I screamed and fisted my threadbare sheets as another orgasm built.

Laz licked and sucked until I was covered in a sheen of sweat and panting deliriously. His fingers replaced his tongue and curled to hit that perfect spot. And then I was detonating, falling into a million pieces and seeing stars.

My breath came out in gasps as aftershocks of my orgasm fluttered through me. Before I had the chance to recover, Lazarus thrust inside of me, filling me completely. Our eyes met and something in my chest rattled awake and reached for him. I was consumed, body, mind and soul, an invisible tether weaving between us and connecting us for what I somehow knew would be forever.

Our eyes stay trained on each other as we moved in tandem. I angled my hips, drawing him deeper inside me then seemed possible. Laz's jaw clenched as he picked up the pace.

"Sweetheart," he grunted. "Fuck. I can't hold back."

"Yes," I breathed. My body pulsating as the pleasure built once again. My eyes closed as his hips slammed into mine, driving himself harder.

"Look at me," he ordered, an otherworldly voice threaded through his own. My gaze flew open, and I gasped at how fucking beautiful my hellhound was. Flames engulfed every inch of him, but not burning me at all, and his eyes were black voids. His finger found my clit as I watched him in amazement. He nuzzled against my neck and as I shattered apart, sharp teeth pierced my shoulder, the combination of pleasure and pain sending me to new heights. I felt his release rock through him and his teeth retracted from my shoulder, his warm, wet tongue sliding over it.

He was muttering something against my skin over and over again and it took a second to realize that he was saying, "mate."

The word would have terrified me before, but now it just felt perfect.

The only thing that would have made it better was if the others were here; a small voice whispered inside of me.

Long moments passed and we stayed there, wrapped in each other's arms. Laz's flames had extinguished with his release, but his skin was still warm, the perfect blanket in the cold cell.

"Are you alright?" Laz purred, licking where he'd bitten me once again. "That was a little unexpected, but I can't say I'm sorry about it." A grin lit up his face, and I couldn't stop myself from kissing him once again.

I snuggled into him, laughing almost giddily.

"Tell me again," he ordered as his hands traced my skin over and over again.

"I love you," I murmured happily as he pulled me even closer.

Lazarus was indeed a drug. And I didn't mind being addicted to him.

CHAPTER 10

KEON

I marched through the hallways, closing in on Selena's cell. I'd spent the whole fucking day appearing like a sleaze-ball while chatting to guards, asking the most awkward questions known to man. One of them even tried to punch me when I asked him to show me his keys. Asshole thought it was a euphemism for something else. Anyway, it was a mistake he now regrets. Hell I wasn't going to get anywhere searching this way.

Considering I couldn't find Alaric anywhere else, I figured I might discover one of them with Selena. And the moment I rounded the corner and entered her prison room, I'd been correct.

She was on her bed, crossed-legged, sitting across from Alaric, and the two of them were playing cards.

I stormed inside, not loving the way he looked at her. I wanted to be the one sharing that moment with her. Sure, Selena had her sights set on more than just me, but it was a damn hard pill to swallow. My instinct was to rip them to shreds for even looking at her, but the choice wasn't mine now, was it? She wanted these men around her, so I had to find a way to accept them if I wanted a part of her.

I groaned inwardly, unable to believe I'd ever conceded this way. But I couldn't bear to lose Selena either, so that meant making sacrifices. And if any of these assholes hurt her, I'd be the first to teach them a fucking lesson.

"Keon," she said, looking up at me. "Everything alright?"

I threw my arms in the air. "How the hell am I supposed to track down the key?" I mumbled more to myself. "I've talked to every guard and there's nothing. And the ones I suspected might be lying, I went and searched their lockers and belongings. Still nothing. You've got to give me more to go on here."

Alaric twisted around to look at me, and for the first time, the prick wasn't judging me. "Have you tried your demon mojo? This is no ordinary key, you know."

"I fucking know it's not a normal key." Though, did he have a point about the demon element?

"It kind of makes sense," Selena answered while climbing off of the bed and stretching her back. My gaze fell to the sweet sliver of skin across her stomach where her black tee lifted. She's so fucking beautiful. If I was sitting around with her, doing nothing, I'd be laid back too. I glared at Alaric, who reclined in the bed, watching my girl as well.

"Like I said." He turned his attention to me. "We don't know who hid the stone in here, so it could have been some demonic fucker. What if the key's invisible?"

"So, I'm supposed to go all hellish on them, scare them

to death, set alarm bells off to see if maybe my demon side senses the key?"

He shrugged. "That sounds like a plan."

I scowled. "Like hell it does. What if I can't bring my demon back? Have you thought of that?" My voice climbed, but Selena's soft hand on my arm dissolved my rising temper.

"What can I do to help? Should we come with you?"

I shook my head. "That won't help."

Her fingers stroked across my inner wrist and I was finding it was difficult to concentrate or remember why I'd let things get me so angry.

"Keon, maybe it's worth giving Alaric's suggestions a try. It makes sense that they wouldn't leave the key lying around for the taking, so it has to be concealed. Maybe the trick is to concentrate on guards who've been here the longest." When she looked at me with her beautiful eyes, I stood no chance of saying no. "And you have to unleash your demon, I will bring you back. I will do anything it takes to return you to me, I give you my word." She pressed herself closer to me, lifting herself on her toes, her breasts against me were all I could focus on. "I love you and would never let your demon claim you."

I cupped the sides of her head and kissed her with a heated passion, my heart banging in my chest that I'd do anything she wanted, while my head was still worried about losing control. But who said I couldn't allow my beast to feast on a soul or two along the way if anyone caused me any problems?

Her kiss burned me up, and she moaned, her fingers gripping the collar of my uniform with urgency. My mind buzzed with idea of walking her to the wall, ripping her pants off, and fucking her. That would help me calm the hell down. I had no idea when I'd fallen so deeply under her spell, but I was completely hers.

Alaric cleared his throat loudly, and Selena straightened in my arms, breaking our mesmerizing kiss.

"You got a problem?" I asked him.

"Yeah, you're wasting time delaying the inevitable. We need that fucking key."

I cursed under my breath when Selena pulled from my arms. "He's right. Sorry that we have to dump this on you," she told me.

"You're the only person I'd risk everything for." Even risk my demon unleashing and me losing control. Sure, I had this.

I straightened my shoulders, then cracked my neck. "Back to it then." I spun on my heels and marched out of there, well aware that this was something only I could do, so I'd make it work.

In my head, I'd already calculated how many guards had been working at Nightmare Penitentiary for over twenty years. I figured that was as good a place to start as any and helped eliminate most of the guards. And when I roughly went through it in my mind, they came to fifteen guards. Still a lot, but better than a couple of hundred.

My footsteps hit the concrete floor hard as I rapidly retraced my steps. I marched right past two pricks beating up on one of their buddies... an even bigger asshole. Let them attack him for all I cared. I had other issues to deal with right now.

The first point of call was the schedule register in the main staff office to see who was in what part of the prison at this time of the day, and who was working today. Once

I checked the staff list, I made a quick mental note of the first five guards to track down, then I hightailed it out of there and down the hall just.

I passed the staff kitchen, then I paused and back-tracked, doing a quick sweep of who was in there... and bingo. Barry was in the back, opening up the fridge, and then pulled out his yogurt and returned to the main lunch table. The guy's been in this place for thirty years, so he was a perfect candidate.

"Barry," I said, strolling deeper into the room. "Still on the yogurt diet?"

Someone else in the room sniggered.

"I swear by it," he said. "Since my missus started me on this, I feel more energetic than I have in years." He peeled open the lid of the vanilla-flavored yogurt tub and began eating like his life depended on it.

Reaching the fridge, I peered inside, needing something to make me look like I was having my lunch break, so I randomly grabbed the first container on the top shelf and went to sit next to him.

Two other guards stared at me. Newbies. And I knew the shit that was spread about me being dangerous. Good.

"Boo," I bellowed at them both suddenly, and they jolted in their seats.

Barry howled with laughter, while the two youngsters made quick work of getting out of there.

"These new guards are so stupid and gullible," Barry told me. "They actually believe the rumors about you. Maybe you can make some up about me and then they'll stop pestering me."

I laughed. *Barry, if only you knew the truth.*

I reclined in my seat, turning my attention to my

coworker, seeing we were now alone. My mind calculated the best way to do this. Do I just turn into my beast in front of him, freak him the fuck out, and see if I could sense the key? Yeah, that's stupid. I didn't want to terrify him or out myself. I preferred people thinking the shit said about me was outrageous gossip.

"What'd you bring?" he asked me.

I stared at him confused at first, unsure what he was babbling about.

His gaze dipped to the red lunch container in front of me on the table. Right, my lunch.

"Ah, you know. The usual boring stuff." I lifted the lid to find three cheese sticks, a small potato, a spoon, and a small tub of Betty Crocker's Whipped Chocolate Frosting.

What the actual fuck! Someone eats this shit for their lunch?

"That's an interesting diet," Barry said, checking out the stupidest meal in the world. I poked the potato to make sure it was at least cooked. It was soft, so that was something. But nothing in this lunch box made sense.

"How does that all work?" Barry asked, then stuffed his mouth with a big spoonful of yogurt, watching me.

My first instinct was to throw the whole thing at him for making that annoying slurping sound as he ate. But instead, I found myself honestly more intrigued by who would think these three items would make a meal.

"My roommate is playing a prank on me," I finally said, closing the lid and pushing the thing away from me.

Barry nodded. "Don't worry. My wife has me into some weird shit, too. Whenever she makes chicken soup, she puts a dollop of vanilla ice cream into it to cool it down. I looked at her like she'd gone mad the first time she did it, but you know what? It was delicious, and now I add it all the time. So, don't let me stop you. You go ahead and eat your cheesy potato dipped in chocolate."

I glared at him, deciding I had enough of this bullshit conversation and freaky food. So, I shot to my feet, the chair scraping across the tiled flooring. I grabbed the lunch box and went to the fridge. "I'm not hungry."

Barry was ranting about food, but I'd tuned out. I opened the fridge, tossed the damn box inside there and shut the door hard. With my back to Barry, who kept slurping and eating with his mouth open, I opened my floodgates and called to my beast. A shiver of dread wormed down my throat at how open and vulnerable we were, but I'd make this quick and not let out the beast completely. He pulsed under my skin, a deep guttural snarl ripping past my throat.

"What in the world is that," Barry asked, turning toward me.

Panic struck as fur raced down my arms. I stormed up behind him before he had the chance to turn around, and I shoved my hand to the back of his head and banged it down on the table. Yogurt splattered and went every-where, but my old friend was out cold. He'd be fine. And with my rush of adrenaline, I welcomed my beast, only partially allowed him to peer out. My skin pricked, the flesh down my back already splitting from his need to escape, to devour this man's soul. Except I didn't want Barry dead. No matter how annoying he was.

Fighting my demonic side, I hissed between my teeth, holding the fucker back, but it was as easy as holding the gates shut to a ramming elephant.

So, I hurried and placed my now taloned hand on Barry's shoulder, my sharp nails digging in, breaking flesh. I stumbled on my feet as the beast slammed inside me trying to escape. "Sonofabitch."

But the longer I held onto Barry, the more I knew he had nothing on him. There was no buzzing, no glow, no reaction. I wrenched my hand free and staggered backward to catch myself as I shoved the beast back deep inside me.

Gasping for air, I stood still for a moment, unsure how good of an idea it was to tease the thing inside me. I'd fed him a soul last night just to be sure he was sated, but that clearly did fuck all.

Shaking off the nerves, I had to stop being so chicken shit and just get this over with.

"Sorry buddy," I said to Barry who had his head on the table looking like he'd fallen asleep in his yogurt.

I took off and was long gone, making my way to where the next guard worked. Lucas Smith. He was close to sixty but one of the toughest guards in here. respected the way he took crap from no one. Plus, he was one of the first few who showed me the ropes when I started my first day, along with some tricks on dealing with the Warden's rules.

The corridor along the top floor was quiet today, and cold. The farther one got from the pit of the prison, the cooler it was in this place.

I passed a few inmates, others remained in their cells, then I took a sharp right and hurried toward the staff communal area when I found no sign of him wandering the halls.

Before I even reached the door, a familiar moaning and slapping sound found me... and it was coming from the guard's room. I smirked. Someone was having a damn good time.

That didn't stop me from pushing open the door slowly and peering inside, only to find Lucas buried deep inside a small redhead he had bent over the table. Her cries were one of arousal, and she loved every damn second of it. I watched for a few moments because, hey, someone was fucking. And I loved to watch. Whoever said they didn't were damn liars. Her ass jiggled each time he slammed into her, her orange prison pants down around her ankles. My thoughts flew to Selena and how much I craved to be buried inside her instead of grilling guards.

Which reminded me of the task at hand. I wasn't going in there yet, so I'd come back later.

Just then the red-haired turned her head in my direction. We locked eyes, and she grinned, loving that she was caught. Fuck, that was hot... and now my cock twitched even more for my girl.

Retreating, I shut the door and made my way down to the bottom levels for the next guard. I stepped out of the elevator, down near the furnace, and a wall of heat collided into me. It didn't take long till I started sweating, and to have my clothes stuck to me. Hell, I hated it down here.

I went right past the doorway into the furnace room and instead went into the hallway where inmates didn't see the light of day for months at a time. This was their punishment for breaking rules in the upper sectors. Sucked to be them.

At the end of the dimly lit corridor, I spotted Nick with his back to me, walking down the hallway. Short white hair and stocky, the man preferred working these lower sections of the prison. And everyone knew why... he was a sexual fucking psychopath, he attacked women. He'd been caught raping one, but the Warden said there had been no actual proof, so instead of punishing him, he reassigned and put him down here to work. Fucking idiots.

We were alone... if you excluded the prisoners in their cells. Which I did.

On silent steps, I closed the distance between us, and within several strides, I called to my beast once more. Sweat dripped down my back.

He suddenly paused in front of a cell and reached for the keys on his belt. Yep, down here, everything was old school; seeing as this was the old part of Nightmare Penitentiary. Without even looking my way, Nick pressed the key into the keyhole. This was my chance.

But instead of just a sliver of my beast, the demon shoved out of me with a vengeance; I stood no chance this time. I clenched my teeth, shuddering on the spot. My skin split, making way for fur as horns started to push out of my temples, hurting like a bitch.

Panic struck just as hard and fast, seeing there were cameras at the end of the hallway.

So, I lunged forward, slamming into Nick's back, both of us bursting into the cell.

The woman inside the room screamed at our explosive entrance. The sound was music to my ears as I fought to not lose complete control of the beast. I trembled with the inner fight. All the while, Nick groaned and bucked beneath me.

I rolled quickly to my feet, and when Nick looked at

me as he got up, his expression paled. "Who the fuck are you?"

My mouth opened, but only a guttural growl escaped. What caught my attention, though, wasn't the terrified woman cowering in the corner or even Nick looking ready to bolt from the room. It was the way his chest was glowing bright blue through his clothes, right in the center, looking like he'd swallowed a huge metal key.

Fuck yes!

I forgot everything else then and loosened my hold on my demon, whispering to him to get the key from Nick's chest.

And then I leapt forward. The corners of my eyes darkened and suddenly I lost all sensation of my body, and watched the events as if I were sitting on the sideline.

Nick went down so fast... he never stood a chance. The woman kept screaming out of pure shock. But my guess was that Nick was coming in here for more than a friendly visit, so he deserved what he got.

The attack was vicious, and I wished more than anything I could be more involved. I'd always hated Nick, and I felt no pity for his demise, not when it stopped his assaults on women and when it got me the key I needed to help Selena. She was my priority over everything else.

My demon slashed Nick's throat first to silence his screams. Blood splattered everywhere. Then he shoved a clawed hand into his chest, breaking ribs. Next thing I knew, the beast wrenched an ancient-looking skeleton key out of the fucker's chest cavity. Blood and bits of flesh slid off the magical artifact, and I smiled on the inside that I'd found it.

The beast opened his mouth and inhaled deeply,

drawing into him... into us, Nick's soul. It was a wisp, barely noticeable, and looked like a thread of mist. It felt like the most incredible warmth sliding through our body, rejuvenating every inch of us.

In the next moment, I was turning toward the female prisoner crouched in the corner, tears streaming down her cheeks. And that familiar hunger rose through me again, the one that belonged to the demon.

Panic flared, curling around my insides, knowing where this was going. I thrust forward before he could fight back, slipping back into the driver's seat. My body convulsed as the fur and horns receded.

But the bastard fought within me, my whole body shuddering as it tried to take me over once more.

"Not this time," I growled, and rapidly drove him to the darkest recesses of my mind.

I pushed myself to my feet and wiped the blood off my face with my sleeve. Tucking the key into the front pocket of my pants, I glanced down to the mess on my shirt. "Shit!" I hastily unbuttoned it. My hands shaking as my demonic side continued to push relentlessly. I gritted my teeth, tensing all over, trying to hold him back. I turned my shirt inside out and put it back on... it looked dirty this way, but not bloody, and in the dimly lit corridors no one would know, right?

Turning to the crying girl, I said, "Shut the door and I'll return to clean this mess. I promise I won't hurt you."

She nodded, shaking. "I-I p-promise I won't say a thing."

With my demon still fighting me for release, I darted out of the room, kicked the door shut behind me, and sprinted down the hallway. I kept bumping into the wall each time the beast shoved against me. He was pissed that I stopped him from feeding. Greedy fucker. One soul wasn't enough, apparently.

Keeping to the shadows, I kept running, planning on returning to my room, but only when I looked up did I realize I'd gone in the opposite direction and ended up at Selena's cell.

Alaric, the beast growled in my mind. With that single word a storm of jealousy flared to life in my body; along with thoughts of what he was doing in that room with her. Kissing her. Fucking her. Fire clawed at my chest, or was that my demon?

Fuck, I couldn't tell anymore, but my legs never stopped moving. I had to stop Alaric... I had to stop myself.

Bursting into Selena's prison cell, I skidded to a stop at the end of the bed. I was sucking in heavy breaths, sweat dripping down my back, yet all I felt was a raging fury within me. Striking me so hard and fast that I stumbled on my feet.

Selena was on her feet, coming to me, her expression petrified. Alaric was at her back, pulling her away from me.

He wants her all for himself, my beast growled in my mind.

I shuddered, holding myself back while every fiber in my body screamed that I just had to make Alaric pay already. Every breath was a struggle, my heart thundering in my chest.

Seething, I shook myself. *Get a hold of yourself.*

"Keon, get the fuck out of here," Alaric snarled, facing me, not backing down.

Something inside me snapped, and I went for him. Unbearable anger steamrolling through me.

I collided with him, shoving my hands into his chest, sending him back. He stumbled to catch himself when a small hand pressed to my chest.

"Stop!"

I looked down at Selena, felt her hand trembling, and saw terror in her eyes. But she never backed down.

"I'm here for you, Keon. Please don't do this. Just listen to my voice."

She was all I heard, nothing else. All I sensed was the warmth of her hands now on my shoulders, sliding up my neck; and holding the sides of my head.

"I'm here for you. Come back to me, Keon." Her voice quivered, and she leaned in close.

A shadow fell over us. "Selena," Alaric warned.

I jutted my head up, a snarl rolling out of my throat, my lips peeling back for him to back away.

"I've got this," Selena yelled, never taking her eyes off me.

When I refocused on her, my world seemed to melt away. The room blurred, and only the two of us existed. Her mouth moved, and I heard her voice telling me to calm down.

That sweet voice was a song in my ears, and it made me forget everything else. It wasn't just me she affected so thoroughly, but my beast, too. I sensed him soften within me, withdrawing. I had known my demon found himself drawn to Selena. It wasn't just me who saw her as mine, but he did as well. Here I was ready to spill Alaric's blood. I was dangerous as fuck, and she didn't fear me but cared for my wellbeing.

If there was ever a moment when my defenses weakened, it was now. My world depended on her, my life entwined with hers. She was everything to me, so how could I ever not bow down to her.

The beast's hunger swallowed me, but he knew she wasn't to be harmed. I held onto Selena, well aware she depended on me. My legs gave out, and I dropped to my knees before her. She looked me in the eye and leaned in to kiss me, our mouths clashing. Our worlds united, and I forgot everything but the softness of her lips, the warmth of her arms, the promise of her love.

Only when she broke our kiss did I realize that I could no longer sense the heavy darkness in my veins. My beast has subsided without a battle with my beauty, our beauty.

"How are you feeling?" she asked while running a hand over my brow, pushing back loose strands of hair. "You had me scared there for a moment."

"I'm feeling better than I have in a long time," I answered, unsure whether or not that had anything to do with the soul the demon had just consumed; or that I still floated on the ambrosia of having someone as beautiful as Selena who loved me. I'd lived without love my whole fucked up life, so this was new and absolutely everything I'd ever wanted. I'd fight the devil himself to keep Selena by my side.

"About fucking time," Alaric mumbled.

I got to my feet and turned to Alaric. For too long, I'd wanted nothing more than to take him down for being near Selena, but I'd seen the way he stared at her like she meant the world to him. Fuck, I understood that feeling so well that it choked me. "Thanks for keeping her safe while I was gone."

Instead of a jerky response, he gave me a nod, an accepting gesture that said more than words. It told me that, like me, he was ready to accept that Selena was too important for either of us to ever give her up. If she wanted us all, then we'd make this somehow work.

I stuck my hand into the front pocket of my pants and pulled out the key. I uncurled my fingers and presented it to them. "One down, one to go."

CHAPTER 11

SELENA

I looked up at Seth. My gorgeous fae who stood in front of me, grasping my hands in his. It hurt my heart with each passing day to know he kept getting beaten, that we were apart, but the potion from Nova had eased his pain, which meant everything to me.

After Keon had found the key, it finally felt like we were making progress, that maybe we'd find this magical stone the Warden wanted. I should be shouting with excitement, yet part of me struggled to celebrate just yet when I'd been beaten down so many times that I forgot what it felt like to win for a change.

"Why do you look so upset?" Seth asked.

I shook my head instantly, my thoughts spinning. "How can I be sad when I'm around you," I reassured him and glanced outside the door of Seth's cell to where Keon stood guard. But our time was limited. Keon was taking a huge risk letting me visit Seth without the Warden's consent. I stared back into Seth's eyes, my heart beating faster, the ache of wanting him free from his punishment echoing in my mind. "We don't have much time."

"What's going on?"

"We found the key," I explained, smiling, and when his mouth curled into a grin, I beamed on the inside. I lived off seeing him happy, which was why I knew I'd fallen so hard for him. I cared so much for him that it physically hurt.

Seth tucked my hair behind an ear, saying, "That's fantastic. We're halfway there." I told him about the fun Keon had in tracking down the key and how incredibly well it had been concealed in a guard's chest.

"That's rather clever," he mused.

I then leaned into his touch, moving closer to him, my heartbeat drumming faster with a desperate need to drag him to his bed, where we could chat and kiss and laugh for hours. Where things felt normal, except nothing in my life was even close to normal, now was it?

"Except, we now need to find the scroll case to open with the key, and Alaric suggested you may know where we can find it. It's magical, so I guess you're the most magical of us all." I shrugged, feeling silly assuming he'd know all things relating to enchantments, but it wasn't like the rest of us knew.

His lips pinched to the side as his gaze drifted upward while he thought. All I could do was lose myself in how beautiful he was, how I winced internally at seeing the red welts across his arms and his neck from the whippings. How I knew, despite how bad they looked, he no longer felt the agony.

But behind his eyes, there was a darkness, like even he knew it was a temporary fix. And like me, he must struggle to believe that after so much, a happy ending was impossible. Except, I couldn't keep thinking that way, and I couldn't allow Seth to resign to it either.

"A dragon," he finally said, breaking me from my thoughts. "I haven't heard any word of a scroll case, but I did once learn that the best place to hide something in Nightmare Penitentiary to never be found was in the dragon's lair deep down in the pit."

My words didn't come at first. Yeah, of course, there'd be dragons in here, why not when every other kind of creature existed? But dealing with one was a terrifying prospect. "Are you sure?" I asked.

"Back in my realm, scrolls were used to carry important documents. As such, they were elaborately decorated with gold, gemstones, and the king's seal. The case itself was highly prized for the wealth that went into it, so where else would someone conceal such a valuable item that wouldn't be easy to hide?"

"With a dragon," I murmured back. "It makes sense, I guess, but shit, a dragon?" My voice climbed a bit too high, drawing Keon's attention as he glanced over his shoulder at us. I met his gaze, and he gave me a quick nod that said, *hurry.*

Seth dragged me closer and whispered, "Dragons are deadly but can be lured to sleep if you can find a way to do so. I couldn't bear it if anything were to happen to you, so let one of the other guys carry out this mission, understand."

"I don't want any of them to get hurt either."

His lip pinched, but he kissed my brow. "They are more experienced in dealing with monsters, and when a dragon turns, there will be nothing that can stop it.

Maybe Keon can aid in getting me out to help execute the mission."

I was at a loss for what to say. The fear in his words scared me... if the dragon terrified him, then was this a death mission for anyone who tried it?

Keon, Alaric, and Laz swirled in my mind. Putting them in front of such danger for the chance to gain more time to be together scared me. They didn't have to risk their lives, but they would insist on it, just as Seth would if given the chance to escape his prison cell.

"I can't have you harmed," Seth told me, his lips finding mine. I kissed him back desperately, like somehow I'd find the answer in his passion. In truth, I gripped onto his arms, wanting to forget the constant danger and instead discover more about Seth, let him claim me over and over.

He kissed with desire, with dominance, with a reminder that I was his. I shuddered at my growing desire, at the thought of him stripping me and climbing on top of me, his weight pressing our bodies together, skin to skin. Just the thought of having him pushing inside of me, spreading my legs, giving myself completely to him made my entire body flutter.

"I miss you so much," I whispered against his mouth.

"Selena, we gotta go, now!" Urgency speared through Keon's words.

I pulled back from Seth, our kiss broken, my heart stinging each time we parted. "I'll be back as soon as I can," I said. Yet my hands remained flush against his powerful chest, as I wasn't ready to part from him. Something in his eyes glinted, reminding me of the brightest stars in the night sky.

"Be safe, my love," he said as he clasped my hand and brought it to his mouth. "I already miss you."

I was breathless, not wanting to go, but when Keon called my name again, I moved from Seth and ran out of his cell. Keon made quick work of shutting the door just as another guard marched in our direction.

"What are you doing here?" he snarled at Keon.

"I'm returning her to her room." Keon didn't wait for a response, but grabbed my arm and hauled me alongside him down the hallway. Once we were out of sight of the other guard, Keon dragged me down a side passage filled with shadows. "Did I hear Seth say a dragon?"

I nodded. "Do you know where they keep it?"

"Yes, but everyone, including the guards, are terrified of it. It's locked up in a pit that's been blocked off. The only way the Warden has kept it under control was to place a mountain of treasure down there with the beast."

His words raced through my mind as I pictured a dragon sitting on a pile of gold, watching for anyone who came to steal it.

"Seth said we need to put it to sleep, and I know someone who can help us with that," I finally said.

"Then we go there now."

I looked at him, my mind trying to work out where Nova's cell was located, seeing as I had never actually been to it. So, I told Keon everything I knew about her and he closed his eyes. When they sprung open, he nodded. "Sector 5D. We keep a few of the magic folk there together."

Next thing I knew, we were speeding through the prison, along hallways, shoving past inmates, and in no time we stopped outside an empty cell. It didn't look much different to mine. Cramped with a cot and toilet in the back, a few books and clothes scattered on a thin shelf, and sad looking. Everything had that depressing feeling.

"She's not here, so we wait?" I suggested.

"Are you looking for me?" Nova's soft voice asked from behind us almost instantly. I spun around, as did Keon, and we found her, chewing gum, wearing a black tank top and orange overalls rolled down to her waist.

"I have a favor to ask," I said instantly.

She glanced over to Keon in his uniform, blinking at him, seeming unsure what to make of his presence. "You're one of her lovers, right?" she asked brazenly, staring at Keon, her question taking me by surprise.

"Yes, he's with me," I confirmed. "You can trust him. We just need your help with something."

"Selena is everything to me," Keon interjected to make his point, which came with an underlying threat that she better not try anything.

"Okay, let's talk inside." She lifted her chin to her cell, and we filed into the tiny space.

"What's going on?" she asked, keeping her eyes trained on Keon. I didn't blame her for not trusting guards. Most of them were assholes, but I was starting to think that wasn't the reason why she looked at him so intensely. "I've heard some weird shit about you, man," she said to him. "It's hard to tell if it's made up to make people scared of you, or real."

"Consider it real," he answered, darkly. "Now, let's talk about the dra--"

"Everything is real?" Nova continued, her eyes widening. "Even the part where you have two dicks, along with horns, and you love to fuck girls with your horns."

That shocked me and my mouth fell open. I looked from Nova then to Keon, stunned and a little curious to know whether this gossip was true. Well the horn part anyway, since I knew he didn't have two dicks... unless he was somehow hiding one? My gaze fell to Keon's crotch with that thought.

Keon barked a laugh, throwing his head back. "Haven't heard those rumors yet, but I like them."

Nova rolled her eyes, seeming almost disappointed. "Yeah figured they were lies. You know half the girls here fantasize about you and would kill to spend a night with you, right?"

"Let's focus," I insisted while bristling at her words. All the while, Keon grinned like the Cheshire Cat.

"I'd like to hear more," he teased.

I elbowed him, and he laughed in that way that made me melt, that called to me. I noticed he affected Nova too, who stared at him with desire in her eyes. A spike of jealousy rose within me. Except I knew Keon loved me and was just teasing me.

I cleared my throat, refusing to be baited by him when I saw him wink my way. "Sooooo," I continued. "Nova, we need a spell, please."

She didn't seem to hear me, but studied the way Keon was flexing his bicep.

When she finally looked at me, she feigned shock at being caught gawking at my boyfriend, then smirked and a strange look flashed in her dark eyes. But it was gone just as quickly as it came.

"A spell you say?" she asked.

"Only if that's ok? I'll pay you."

She made a raspberry type sound with her mouth and rolled her eyes. "Don't be crazy. I still owe you for saving me, so let's have it. What do you need?"

"A sleeping spell," Keon responded.

"For a dragon," I clarified, figuring that would be a different type of enchantment.

Her eyes widened and her mouth slipped into an enormous smile, her white teeth on show. "What are you up two up to that involves a dragon?"

"It's a super long story," I said. "Once it's over, I promise to tell you all about it. So, is that a yes?" I pleaded, looking at her with eagerness.

"Heck yeah, anything for my girl and..." she glanced over to Keon. "And maybe seeing you around this sector a bit more often would be good. Guards don't come here often, and it's not the safest section, you know."

The way she eye humped Keon didn't seem to match her plea for protection, but I decided to let it go as long as we got the spell. Keon was mine, after all.

"I'll check my schedule," Keon answered cockily. I wanted to roll my eyes. Was he actually flirting? He clearly loved the attention.

"Okay, let me get that spell for you then," Nova said. "Wait here and I shouldn't be long. I keep my ingredients in another cell."

"You're doing it now? Doesn't it take a while?"

She laughed at me and patted my arm. "You've been watching too much Harry Potter." Next thing I knew, she sauntered out of the cell and vanished down the hallway.

I turned to Keon, who just shrugged and leaned a

shoulder against the wall, studying me from head to toe. "You think she'll be gone long enough for a quickie?"

I snorted a laugh at him. "After you were flirting with her, nope," I teased him back.

"Babe." He snatched me by the waist, and I was in his arms in a heartbeat. "I only have eyes for you, but you saw the way she looked at me. So, I played the game to get her to help us."

His kiss stole my response. His touch slid across to my back, one hand on my ass, and his arousal nestled against my stomach. "You are the world to me," he whispered against my lips, then licked them. "I've never felt this way about anyone before, and I will destroy whoever stands in my way to hold onto the only thing I need... and that's you, my beautiful girl."

Pressing closer to him, my hands curling around his neck, I said, "You know how to sweet talk me, don't you?"

He winked again in the way that weakened my knees, and this time I pulled him closer and kissed him back to show him exactly how much he means to me, half considering the quickie.

"Can I watch?" Nova suddenly asked.

I jumped away from Keon, breaking from our kiss as I wasn't expecting her back so quickly.

"Already done?" Keon asked.

"Yep." She stepped into the prison cell and lifted her fist, holding a small string-tied bag.

"Wow, that was fast. Are you sure it's going to work against a dragon?"

She nodded. "I have a batch of sleeping potion premade since it's my biggest seller here. So, I just added more of my mojo and additional ingredients to match the strength of a dragon." She opened her palm, and I stared at the small black bag. "When you reach the creature, pour the contents in your palm, and blow it in his face."

My mouth fell open. "I wasn't really expecting to get that close to his face or his huge teeth," Keon added.

"He has a point," I said.

"The beauty about this is that I added a pinch of ground-up pixie wings, and with a small sprinkle of my power, you can do this from across the room and the powder will swish to the dragon. Just whisper the word, *dragon*, before you blow the ingredients toward him."

It seemed to make sense, I guessed, but what did I know about magic? Not much.

"But," she continued, and that was the sucker punch I'd been waiting for.

"But?" I asked.

"Dragons are unruly beasts and there are no guarantees how long this potion will last. That's why anyone crazy enough to face a dragon is never seen again. But I'm sure you know what you're doing."

I swallowed over the boulder forming in my throat, and I glanced up at Keon. He shrugged and took the magic pouch from Nova before tucking it into his pocket. "We'll be fine." Taking my hand, he then swiveled and began pulling me from the room.

"Thanks, Nova. I'll come see you afterward."

She nodded. "I hope so." The worry in her voice troubled me. Once outside in the hallway, I cut Keon a concerned look. "Maybe we should have asked for a different spell. Like one to tie up the dragon, bind his mouth or something stronger than a sleeping potion?"

"Your friend was right, in that the spell may not last

long so we have a short time to get this done. But with dragons being such powerful creatures born from the ashes of magic itself, any spell we used would be just as limited. So, I'd rather take my chances sneaking around a dragon who doesn't see me, than taking him face to face if he snaps out of his restraints."

I nodded hesitantly. "So, we get Alaric and Laz to join us?"

He paused mid-step and spun toward me. "Selena, you aren't coming."

"Yes, I am." I stood my ground, lifting my chin. I wasn't backing down. "None of you can take on a dragon, so this mission has nothing to do with brawn. It's about lots of eyes searching for the scroll as quickly as possible. So, the more of us there are, the faster we can get out of there before the dragon wakes up. Maybe we should even see if Seth can come along, too?"

He didn't respond right away, his lips pinching. Clearly, he hated my suggestion about me coming along, but he also couldn't deny I was correct.

"I don't know if I can swing Seth joining us, but I'll see what I can do. For now, I'll leave you with Alaric while I go roundup Laz, then we can all work out our plan of action."

"Laz is starting to grow on you, isn't he?" I asked, smirking, loving to see the guys getting along.

"As much as a mushroom grows in the darkest corner of a cave."

I nudged him. "He's a decent guy, you know."

Keon nodded, but didn't respond. His hand squeezed mine, and we were off again, moving without pause. The whole time, my stomach grew tighter and tighter about tackling a dragon. As much as I fought to join the others on this mission, a shiver kept tracking down my spine that we were walking into a death trap.

* * *

STANDING IN THE DARK HALLWAY, I couldn't stop shaking. Wisps of smoke curled out from under the door as we neared. It smelled like an entire forest was burning.

A thunderous roar sounded, shaking the floor beneath my feet.

"Shit!" I murmured under my breath, unsure about this plan.

"Are you certain the scroll is in there?" Laz asked.

"Seth said it might be, and it's the only clue we have," Keon responded. "So, we're going to follow through."

"It makes sense, though. Where else would you hide something you don't want anyone to find but under a dragon's ass," Alaric said.

"Yeah, well, as long as it's not in his ass, or ends in us being barbecued," Laz added.

Keon narrowed his gaze at him. "Fuck man, why did you have to say that ass bit? Why would a scroll be up a dragon's ass? Now I can't get the image out of my head."

Laz shrugged, focusing on the smoke wafting out from beneath the door. "Have you forgotten where we are? Anyone could get to the treasure, but if it's inside the animal, well... And don't forget where the key was hidden."

"Shit," Alaric growled.

Laz continued like he hadn't just put the worst image

129

in all our minds. "We put the dragon to sleep and then rush around like crazy searching for a scroll in there?"

"Pretty much," Keon said.

I curled my hand around the pouch in my pocket. "So, if we see the dragon stirring awake, we all get out of there," I reminded them.

"Like fucking rockets," Alaric said, smirking.

I wanted to laugh, but I had sweat rolling down my spine from the dread curling around me.

Keon stepped up to the door, glancing back down the hallway from where we came, then reached for the keypad on the wall. "There is an inner protective room where we feed the beast from. We go in there, then I will open the food hatch and, Selena, you use that opening to cast the spell, okay?"

I nodded, my stomach knotting badly. I had no idea what to expect, and part of me felt like I might pass out from how much I shook.

With a click, Keon unlocked the door and pulled it open.

None of us moved at first. We were all paralyzed with fear while trying to look inside and work out what we were dealing with.

The room was dimly lit. And in front of us, I spotted a section encased in plexiglass keeping us safe from the dragon.

"Hurry," Keon ushered us, and we all hurried inside, after which he shut the door.

Only once I'd stepped inside did the true magnitude of the dragon's lair come into view. We were standing on a platform with metal steps running down from our right into the enormous cavern. So big that I couldn't see where it started or ended in any direction. It just kept going and going, swallowed by shadows. Sporadically, I could see huge stone pillars that looked charred and battered. Hell... how were we going to search this place quickly? We needed at least another hundred people.

The ground was littered with what I could only describe as junk. Appliances, furniture, a bathroom tub, and lots of picture frames in varied metallic colors. In fact, everything had that in common. They were burnished in silvers and golds and bronzes.

These weren't treasures. As I surveyed the area, I noticed I couldn't see the dragon.

"Where is it?" Laz whispered.

Suddenly, the platform beneath us shook, and I fell against the railing in front of me.

Alaric's strong arms whipped around my middle, steadying me. He drew me back to stand against his rock-hard chest, while we all stared out, not saying a word.

An explosive blur swept past us from the right, screeching before spitting flames and disappearing into the darkness. It came so fast, and it was enormous, I gasped and lost my breath.

With a thunderous roar, the dragon reappeared from the left and landed in front of us, its head level with us... My knees shook at having a beast whose one eye was the size of my head staring right into my soul. Its dark scales glinted a silvery blue and green color against the wild campfire in the middle of the room, seeming to burn some of the junk in its treasure cave.

Its nostrils flared at the end of his long snout, steam curling upward from the corners of his mouth. Lips curled back, incisor teeth exposed, promising instant death. Curved horns sat amidst a messy mane of black fur that sat around its head, and deep blue hooked claws tipped its leathery wings. It drew its wings tightly against its sides as it studied us.

"All I can think about is that scroll being up its ass," Keon growled. "Thanks for that, Laz."

Laz chuckled, finding amusement, while I couldn't stop looking into the eyes of death. The animal pulled its head back, a torrent of smoke streaming out between razor-sharp teeth.

"Okay, so are we ready?" Keon asked.

"No. I'll never be ready to confront that," I answered truthfully.

The beast drew in an abrupt, deep breath, and in a heartbeat, he roared, the sound ear-piercing. And just on the back of his screech, an explosion of fire burst out from his mouth.

Instinct took me over, and I screamed while covering my head and ducking. I ended up smacking into Alaric who held me in place. "You're safe," he told me.

Like fuck I was... Fire encased the whole enclosure, the heat unbearably painful, and for those few seconds, it felt like the dragon had swallowed us and we were inside its belly.

When the flames died and the dragon pulled back, none of us said a word.

I sucked in each rushed breath, and I looked around to see the ashen look on Laz and Alaric's faces. Keon seemed more in control, but then again, he knew what to expect. I was still coming to terms with... with that beast!

"We don't have much time," Keon reminded us.

I licked my lips and grabbed the pouch from my

pocket, my hand trembling. Finding my bravery, I also found my voice. "Alright then. Let's do this." I didn't believe a word I said, but I wasn't exactly swimming in solutions either to avoid being killed by an inmate.

I moved to join Keon, who was unlocking the food hatch. "It's expecting food," he told me. "So, let's use this opportunity. As soon as I open it, then do your thing."

I wasn't completely confident in my 'thing' seeing I just had Nova hand it over to me with little instruction.

Quickly untying the pouch, I poured the contents into my palm, then quickly stuffed the pouch back into my pocket.

Sweat collected across my lower back. But I'd dealt with enough crap that blowing magic dust into a dragon's face was nothing in comparison.

The dragon seemed to pace in front of the platform, each step pounding the ground. Keon used the moment when the dragon spun from us to pull open a half door, big enough to pass through huge meals, like half a cow, I guessed.

Quickly, I lifted my cupped palm to my lips, my fingers unfurling from over the powdery magic, which was the color of the brightest sunset. With a lungful of air, I whispered, "dragon," then blew the contents out of my hand.

Tiny particles took flight instantly, glinting and looking like tiny firebugs. They seemed to have a life of their own, moving like a swarm of birds in the sky, swirling with purpose, and in this case, the magic was darting toward the dragon.

The beast turned at that moment, just as the magic dust reached its face. It inhaled and started choking and snorting, but the powder was already into its mouth, its nostrils, in its eyes and ears.

Keon hastily shut the feeding door, and we all watched the dragon.

One second it was standing, confused, looking at us. And in the next second, he face-planted into the ground, sending a cloud of dust into the air. The cavern shuddered from the impact.

No one said a word.

We leaned forward to stare down at him.

"Looks like it worked," I said. "Maybe we should wait a bit to make sure?"

A flutter of cool air rushed across the back of my neck, and I glanced over to find Keon had already opened the plexiglass door toward the steps and was rushing down into the cavern. Laz followed.

"This is our chance," Alaric said, his hand in mine and taking me down with him.

"Where in the world do we start?" I asked.

"How long do we have?" Laz added.

"We were told it may not keep the dragon down for long, so quick as fuck is your answer," Keon said.

"Great," Laz responded sarcastically.

"Okay, we each go in different directions and are looking for a scroll case that could hold maps," Alaric explained.

"And it should be obscenely decorated, according to Seth," I added.

"Got it. Something long, thick, and highly prized." Laz winked at me. How could he still joke at a time like this?

"Let's move," Keon ordered. Then everyone scrambled

in different directions, leaving me on the right side of the cavern.

Quick steps took me directly into the chaos of trashy treasures. I kept looking over my shoulder at the dragon, praying it didn't suddenly get up and burn us to a crisp for touching his junk. I kicked something hard and looked down at a freaking toaster. Seriously, this dragon had no clue what real treasure was.

But then again, what was meaningful was in the eye of the beholder, right?

I hurried and started rummaging around, shoving a chair out of my path, my gaze scanning the place for anything that might glint. Anything long and tube-like.

Time seemed to stand still, and I had no clue how long we'd been searching, but I was sweating up a storm. Occasionally, I caught a glimpse of one of the guys, darting through the junk, searching and tossing things around.

I paused near a stone pillar and wiped the perspiration from my brow, staring to where the shadows stole the light. A sense of hopelessness flared over me at how immense the job was considering we weren't one hundred percent sure the scroll was down here in the first place. But while everyone one else searched, I wouldn't give up. I couldn't, so I went back to work.

It wasn't long before I kicked the corner of a couch that stood in my way so hard that I swore I broke my baby toe. The worst pain in the world struck and crawled up my leg, my baby toe feeling like someone had just chopped it off. I muffled a cry, my knees giving out, and I rolled on the ground, reaching for my toe, rocking in place.

Goddamn... stupid... fucking couch. How the hell was

a dragon collecting furniture, anyway? To decorate or to burn. Fuck! My toe throbbed, and it stung so badly tears pooled in my eyes.

"Sleeping on the job?" Laz mocked from somewhere behind me.

I groaned under my breath and twisted toward him when something golden glinted in the corner of my eye right by an open fridge laying on its side. Something I could only see from being low to the ground.

"Bingo!" I murmured under my breath and hurried over on my hands and knees. *Please let it be the scroll case.*

Just then, an earth-shattering roar exploded behind me, the kind that only a terrifying, pissed-off dragon would make.

My heart immediately skipped several beats, then full panic mode settled in my bones.

"Fuck, fuck, fuck," Laz cursed from somewhere behind me.

I darted behind some boxes and curled in to make myself as small as possible. Only when I looked out from my hiding spot did I see the true extent of the trouble we were all in.

Laz hid behind a burned car, about twenty feet from me, his eyes on the beast, then over to me. I couldn't see Alaric, but somehow Keon had made his way back up into the protected plexiglass platform.

I glanced behind me quickly to the open fridge and there sat the freaking scroll case, at least two feet in length, golden decorations all over the outer shell. At the top, a keyhole... I'd hit the jackpot alright, except it might just get me eaten.

Looking up, Keon was gone, leaving the three of us

down here. But he wouldn't do that. He had to be getting help.

Peering out at the dragon. I saw that he was stumbling around, shaking his head. This was my chance. I took a deep breath and lunged for the case. I grabbed it and scurried back to hide behind the boxes because as much as I considered bolting up the stairs while he still appeared out of it, I doubted he would have a problem charbroiling me.

When it unleashed another terrifying roar, this time fire sprouted from its mouth, and I ducked low. *Shit, shit, shit.*

Only when he grew silent again did I look up to find the animal lingering near the platform, meaning we weren't going anywhere, anytime soon. I glanced over to Laz, who stared my way. He was farther from the platform, so he'd have to cross the open area without attracting the dragon's attention to reach me.

I shook my head, then gingerly picked up the scroll case and showed it to him.

He did a small fist pump and smiled. I don't know how long we waited after that, but my legs were cramping from sitting in a curled ball behind the boxes.

A sudden blur came from my right, and I flinched so hard a small cry spilled from my lips.

I quickly slapped a hand to my mouth just as fast.

"Fuck," Alaric's whispered voice came from my left, crouching low behind a laundry basket.

I blinked at him and did a double-take. "What? Where did you...?" I couldn't finish my sentences as shock collided into me. Alaric was next to me.

A thunderous footstep hit the ground, then another.

Alaric placed a finger over his mouth, making a quiet *shhh* sound. Then he pointed to his left, where there seemed to be, amid the collected treasures, a small path that led to the steps.

He shuffled in closer to me, and his eyes were on the scroll case, widening at the sight of our prize. I lifted my gaze to the dragon beating its wings, taking flight.

Fuck, had he seen Alaric moving?

My heart beat faster, and terror gripped me.

Alaric grabbed my wrist and he pulled me to move.

The dragon's roar had me flinching.

I was certain my heart was attempting to burst out of my ribcage. But with Alaric's strength, he forced me to move instead of freezing from fear.

Rapidly, we crawled along the narrow path, and I kept looking over my shoulder, noticing Laz had vanished from his position.

Panic struck, and I glanced around. He was sprinting in the opposite direction, drawing the beast away from us.

"Crap, no." I wrenched against Alaric's grasp on my hand. He paused and glanced back at me, his expression perplexed.

I pointed toward Laz with the dragon flying in his direction.

"Goddamnit." Alaric hoisted himself to his feet, dragging me with him. "Run, gorgeous. Get the hell out of here."

Before I could respond, he shoved me in front of him, then gave me a strong nudge to my lower back. I stumbled forward, then spun back around to find he'd already gone after Laz and the dragon.

I had a complete moment of confusion about what to

do next. Nova came to mind and her spells. Before I knew it, I was racing past the junkyard, leaping over objects, my breaths puffing, my gaze swinging from how far the stairs still lay to where the animal and my men were.

The stairs weren't far.

I could no longer see Laz or Alaric.

But I kept running because all our lives depended on it.

When a shadow fell over me, my stomach knotted, and I threw my arms over my head, hunching forward. For those few moments, I became resigned to the fact that this was it. My moment had come, and any second now, I'd perish into a ball of flames.

But when my end never came, I craned my head up.

The dragon crash-landed in front of the platform, mouth open, staring right at Keon. He stood in the plexiglass room, carrying a massive, frozen turkey. He opened the food hatch and without hesitation hurled the bird at the beast.

In one swipe, it snatched the turkey out of the air, chewing on it, but it was gone in seconds. Keon grabbed another turkey from the large box at his feet. I frantically looked around for my other two men who were racing up behind me, panic in their eyes, and waving for me to go, go, go.

I whipped around and threw myself up the stairs, the plexiglass door swinging open for us.

The dragon's head jutted in our direction in that same moment, fury burning in his eyes.

"Hurry," Keon bellowed, then tossed another turkey at the dragon, which only hit him in the face, then plonked to the ground.

The beast started pivoting away from the front of the large platform, coming around to the side toward us.

My feet scrambled faster. Someone's hands were on my back, pushing me, and Keon was there. He reached and grabbed my arm, and next thing, I was flying into the enclosure, then landed on my hands and knees.

Alaric and Laz threw themselves in right after me just as a burst of fire exploded from the dragon's mouth.

Quick-footed, Keon grabbed the plexiglass door and hauled it shut just as the flames engulfed us.

Huddled around the scroll case, I lowered my head, hating the cracking and snapping sounds, the overbearing intensity of the heat.

Finally, when it subsided, strong hands grabbed me by the waist, and I was off my feet being rushed out of the dragon's cavern.

When my toes touched the floor again, all four of us were in the hallway, the door to the beast locked, and our breaths heaving out of our lungs. All my guys' faces were red and covered in ash, their eyes wild with the terror we'd just escaped.

"Fucking hell, that was close," Laz muttered exactly how I felt.

"Please, let's never do that again," I said.

Keon and Alaric didn't say a word. They were staring at the scroll case in my arms. I glanced down and lifted it in front of me, smiling. "I can't believe we actually found it and survived."

"Can I touch it?" Alaric asked, already stretching his hand out. His fingers stroked the side of the scroll. I wasn't sure if he expected it to affect him, but when nothing happened, he drew his hand away.

"Okay, so where's the key?" Laz asked.

"With me," Keon asked, moving to stand next to me. "Let's get out of here and do this in a safe place."

We all nodded and hurried as far from the dragon as possible. "I really hope whatever we find inside isn't an impossibly difficult treasure map. I mean, what is worse than facing a man-eating dragon?"

No one answered, and that told me everything. Whatever came next might be the end of us.

CHAPTER 12

LAZ

$\mathcal{A}$laric's cell appeared a lot bigger than mine, complete with a table and chairs, a private section for the toilet… was that a minibar? What the fuck? Talk about privileges. Then again, I'd heard enough things about the guy to know most feared him. So, no surprise that the Warden favored him.

But I didn't hate him, and especially not after he'd just saved my skin coming back to save me from the dragon. The more time I spent with Selena and the guys she surrounded herself with, the more I understood why she was drawn to them.

Aside from being fucking scary sonsofbitches, they adored her to a fault… the kind that involved killing anyone who dared touch her. That passion roared inside me, too. From our first time meeting in the mess hall, I knew she was different and the impact she had on me was instantaneous. I fell fucking hard and didn't regret a single thing. And for me, I was in for life with her.

I looked at the open cell door, expecting Keon to

arrive at any moment. He'd apparently put in a request to get Seth out of his cell for some bullshit reason, and it had just been approved. So, he was collecting him to join us. He insisted that since we were dealing with magic, that it made sense to have a powerful fae like Seth with us when we opened the scroll case... just in case. Who the hell knew what we'd find, so we waited for their return.

"Nice room," I said, studying Alaric's bookshelf with books all about history and warfare. That said a lot about him.

"Alaric definitely gets special privileges," Selena told me, our hands grazing, and I took her hand in mine. She was warm to the touch, and I adored the way she'd pressed in against me.

"I don't think so," Alaric answered, and we both glanced over to him lounging at the end of his bed like not much worried him.

"Sure," I said, and Selena smirked at him.

"So, what do you think we'll find in the case?" she asked.

I shrugged. "I'm hoping it's the actual stone. Wouldn't that be nice?"

Alaric in response collected the scroll case lying on the bed next to him and shook it. "Nope, doesn't sound like there's anything inside."

"Shit, it better not be empty," Selena said. "After what we just went through, I'm going to be really angry if we hit a dead end."

"We are finding that stone today," a deep voice said from behind me.

I twisted around just as Seth and Keon entered the room. Selena's breaths hitched, and she dropped my hand, then rushed to Seth, throwing her arms around him. He wrapped her up in his embrace. They exchanged hushed whispers and a kiss. I shouldn't have stared at their moment, but I felt like she belonged to me too, so the intimate time involved all of us. We got to share their reunion.

The passion she held for all the men in this room was undeniable. I'd always been a dominant man who never considered sharing in a million years, but it was funny how when you met the right person, everything changed.

I studied the powerful fae who carried a strong aura that commanded attention. Despite the injuries on his neck and arms, even the stories I'd heard of his beatings, he stood with determination and radiated power. It explained why the Warden had kept such a close guard on him... I suspected out of all of us, Seth could be the most deadly.

"I'm ready to do this," Keon started.

Alaric climbed to his feet and the four of us now stood around Selena, who'd collected the scroll case and had it in her hands. Keon retrieved the key from his pocket and handed it to her. The room fell silent, and we watched intensely as she pressed the key into the lock. It went in all the way, then she twisted it clockwise. A small click sounded, and the top of the scroll case flipped open and clattered to the floor.

I leaned in closer for a look inside the case, as did everyone else. Selena lowered the tube-like case for a better look when a bright green light flicked and shot out of the container.

Selene reared back, still holding onto the scroll case

but all our attention followed the tiny light that was the size of a fly, hovering in front of us.

"What is that?" Selena asked in a breathless whisper.

"Doesn't look like a map to me," Alaric muttered.

"Is it a spell?" Keon added.

"Maybe it's a test?" I said.

Just then, the light zipped away from us and right past Keon and me. Twisting to follow it, the light lingered outside the cell, just hovering there.

"It's a tracking device," Seth said. "We need to follow it quickly."

The moment he said the last word, the light darted to the right into the hallway.

"Shit," I murmured and scrambled out after it. Everyone fell in close behind me. "There it is." I pointed to it curving around a corner down the hallway.

I ran after it... we all did without pause, stampeding past inmates who lunged out of our way at seeing our approach. I moved faster, loving the chase. It had been too long since I'd been out on a true hunt... since being locked up in here, of course. Before that, I hunted every day. But that was a past I wanted to forget, a past tainted with betrayal by my second-in-command after he killed my mate and framed her murder on me. I seethed at the thought and shoved that anger into my determination to destroy him.

The fast, rhythmic thud of my heart picked up the farther we ran. Selena was beside me, and my hand fell to hers, holding onto her. We ran together.

The magical light steered us left and right, and even I lost track of where we were. I kept looking back, swearing we were going in circles.

Hallways grew darker and longer, until we reached the staff elevator in what I finally recognized as the west wing, and as far from our cells as possible. The green light zipped down between the tiny gap, vanishing.

"What the fuck!" Alaric gasped for air.

"It went down," Selena confirmed what we'd all seen, stepping forward, her hand pulling free from me.

Keon jabbed a finger into the button and entered his passcode in the keypad on the wall. The moment the doors opened, we all rushed inside the small space, pressed together like sardines.

"What floor?" Keon asked, staring at the six buttons on the wall.

"Start in the basement," I suggested. "Where else would a magical light go?"

Seeing no one had a better plan, Keon hit the button, and we lurched forward as the elevator jerked and started descending. I rubbed shoulders with Seth, who now held onto Selena to stop her from losing her footing.

In moments, the doors slid open to a dark corridor. No one moved a muscle. There was no sight of the green spark we'd been chasing. Or much light at all, for that matter, in this area.

"What's down here?" Selena asked, sticking her head forward to peer out.

"It's mostly used for storing equipment and anything that has no home, not to mention the Warden keeps a lot of his other collectibles locked away down here, as well."

"Maybe we should burn them all?" Seth suggested, causing everyone to look at him. It wasn't what I expected him to say, and apparently, neither did anyone else.

"I'm with, Seth," Selena piped up when a familiar green

light zipped out into the hallway from the right, taunting us.

"There it is," I called out, taking the lead and rushed out of the elevator, determined to not lose the damn thing again.

* * *

Selena

WE WERE OFF AGAIN, my breathing out of control, and I wiped the sweat from my brow. Just like visiting the dragon, this level of the prison burned with heat.

I kept up to Laz and Keon, who took the lead, Seth and Alaric at my back. It was a strange thing to be surrounded by all four men, to have them all cooperating and not attempting to rip each others' heads off. The danger coming for me seemed to have shaken them, not to mention myself. We'd come this far, so this had to work in my favor.

Rounding a corner, we hit a dead end... or more specifically, a set of doors bolted shut. Keon wasted no time getting them unlocked with the ring of keys attached to his belt. There was no hesitation in him; he was breaking prison rules... his sense of duty went out the window the moment the Warden put a target on my back. His loyalty was to me.

Laz collected my hand in his, and he drew me past the open doors. We emerged into a great hall thrown into darkness. Keon grabbed the flashlight on his belt and flicked on the light, the beam revealing an actual ballroom, complete with chandeliers.

"The fuck!" Alaric bellowed. "Has the Warden been holding dinner parties down here with the demons he makes deals with?"

"It sure looks like it," Seth answered.

"Before the building became a penitentiary, the lower levels were used by the underworld creatures when they entertained non-demonic beings. It was a halfway point," Keon explained.

The green light blinked through the darkness and veered right. We rushed after it until it suddenly vanished. And that was when Keon's beam of light swept over a door.

"I don't think I have a key for this entry," he said, though he still tried some of his keys with no success.

"Move over," Laz commanded.

Keon did just that and moved to the side. Then Laz and Alaric charged to the wooden door, ramming their shoulders into it repeatedly.

Wood groaned, echoing around us. When the door didn't break open, Keon turned and rammed his heel into the wooden door, sending shards of wood flying in every direction. I ducked in case the shards came flinging in my direction.

The green light hovered inside the room. Then before our eyes, it burst into specks of green light and dissolved into lime-green ash, vanishing.

"This has to be it," I murmured in awe, mostly to myself.

Keon took the lead, and I watched intently as he entered the room and his flashlight illuminated a grand black gate that divided the large room in half. It was as if someone had blocked off a portion of the room with metal bars.

I followed Keon, as did the others, and I approached the elaborate gate, the lock made of a skull.

"What's in there?" Alaric asked, and we were all peering inside, holding on to the metal bars as Keon slowly swept the light left and right across the empty cell... until the beam paused on a treasure chest that looked like it came directly out of a pirate movie.

"We found it," Seth breathed. My thoughts exactly.

"We need to get in there," Alaric started, "How do we get in there?" gripping the metal bars tighter in his hands, which reminded me of the key from the scroll case I'd stuffed into my pocket earlier.

"Maybe this key has more than one purpose," I said, gaining everyone's attention. They crowded around me, watching as I inserted the key while holding my breath.

Please let this work, please.

A single drop of sweat rolled down my spine as I wanted this so badly that I was ready to cry. I'd had enough of being everyone's target practice, of always having others beat me down.

This had to work.

I pushed the key in deeper and turned. When the lock clicked open, I exhaled so loudly; I surprised myself. "You did it," Keon announced, his hand on my lower back. He reached in front of me and tugged on the gate. And we all stepped back as it swung open with a moan. Then as one, we stepped inside.

A loud clapping sound came from behind us suddenly, and I whirled around, unsure what was going on.

Nova stood in the doorway to the room, a shoulder leaning against the doorframe, and clapping like a villain.

"What are you doing here? Did you follow us?" I asked while Alaric and Seth stepped toward her, their shoulders bunched up, tension permeating the air.

She lowered her arms to her sides, shadows dancing beneath her eyes, and suddenly the person standing before us wasn't Nova. Well, it was... but her demeanor had changed; it belonged to someone else.

"You are so gullible, Selena," she said. Then moved in a flash right past us like she was made of the wind itself. When I spun around, she was standing beside the treasure chest, the lid open.

And she was clutching a glowing green stone the size of my fist.

She had the Cintamani Stone!

CHAPTER 13

SELENA

"Nova!" I cried out. "What are you doing?" But I knew better... of course I did. I just didn't want to face the truth. She'd been lying to me this whole time. Using me. The pain that bloomed in my chest telling me it was the only explanation for her behavior. My perpetual need for love and friendship would inevitably always lead to my downfall.

It was Seth who stepped forward first, while Alaric shut the gate, locking us all in with her.

"Who are you?" Seth asked, tilting his head to the side, his gaze piercing Nova like he saw something none of us did.

"How are you feeling, lover-boy?" she replied, smirking. "I did you a favor, helping to eliminate the pain after your beatings."

"And for that I am thankful. Now hand over the stone, and no one will hurt you." He stuck his hand out, palm facing up, his fingers unfurling outward.

"I think I'm going to keep it." Nova was tossing the

stone up and down in her hand. My heart stopped every time she did that, feeling like she played with my very life each time she threw it into the air.

"Why are you here doing this?" I asked, stepping forward. "I thought we were friends."

"You call it friends, I call it keeping my enemy close," she sneered.

Her words confused me, and I blinked at her, unsure what she was talking about. There was something seriously wrong with her. I could see it in her eyes. They were darker than normal, and the facial expression twisted into one of a permanent frown. She was definitely not the Nova I knew.

"Why the enemy?" Keon asked. "What has she done? Or have you finally decided to eliminate Selena and collect the bounty the Warden promised?"

Nova was shaking her head. "Pffff, as if. I could have taken her out already if that was the case. Nope, she was dumb enough for me to use for something else I needed." Her gaze fell to the stone in her hand, the green glowing under the faint light from Keon's flashlight.

I swallowed hard at her words. She'd used me this whole time to get the stone? But that didn't make sense. So many things didn't add up. "I don't understand? When we first met, it was a pure coincidence."

"Was it?"

My stomach rolled at hearing those words, and a wave of sickness rose to the back of my throat. "Who the fuck are you?" I demanded.

"Five against one," Laz butted in. "Speak up because my patience is close to snapping."

We were facing her in a semi-circle, but I'd seen her

power and by the cocky expression on her face, the threat didn't frighten her.

Suddenly the air in the room dropped several degrees, and a shiver ripped down my spine. My quickening exhales came out as mist, and before us, Nova was twitching.

A flash of white came from her eyes, then in a heartbeat, something white slid from the side of her as if she were splitting in two. Except that wasn't right... something was stepping out of her... Nova slumped forward, her shoulders curled, her face pale as death as if she was so close to the end, she barely clung to life.

And next to her stood the ghost who'd been trying to kill me, to take me over. It stood before us. *Are you fucking kidding me?* I seethed and my hands curled into fists as everything started to make sense. She set me up, pretending to be my friend... just to get close to me. She hated me for exorcising her out of my body, and her last words stayed with me.

You'll pay for this.

She'd taken over this poor woman to come after me, to make me pay. The ghost was a psychopathic stalker.

Her skin was a shimmering, barely translucent silver, just like before, as was her black hair pulled back into a bun and parted down the middle. She wore her Gothic black Victorian dress again, and the tightness in her grin sent shivers down my arms.

"Are you serious?" I practically screamed as frustration tore through me. "What is your problem with me?"

And in a flash, she shoved herself back into Nova, who stumbled on her feet and gasped back to life. It didn't take her long for her to regain her posture and for color to blossom back into her cheeks. I didn't know what to believe anymore.

"We kill her now!" Alaric growled.

"You touch me, and I'll destroy the stone," Nova stated, gripping the green stone in her hands and lifting it over her head, ready to smash it to the ground. "Then how will you save your little, Selena?"

I sucked in a sharp breath with the terrifying realization that she knew about the Cintamani Stone. Getting that stone was the only way to protect myself against the Warden... and Julian.

"What do you want?" I asked reluctantly, when my first instinct was to tell Alaric to rip her apart.

"You," she snapped back. "Give yourself willingly to me. That's all I ask."

"Like fuck she will," Keon roared.

Laz bristled beside me. "Do you think any of us will stand by and let you do that?"

Nova smirked. "I don't care what the rest of you want."

Seth was surprisingly quiet. He watched Nova as a predator studied his prey. And I couldn't figure out what he was thinking or planning. All the guys' expressions were tight and flared with rage.

Keon cleared his throat, drawing her attention. "Let's come to another arrangement," Keon suggested, staring at her with a calm demeanor, which was the opposite of him. "You take me however you want in exchange for the stone. And I'm not talking about a one-time deal either."

I stared at Keon; he had to be kidding. He wouldn't do that, right? My heart lurched into my throat at the thought of him with her for my sake. I couldn't bear the image of him touching anyone else when my heart had already claimed him.

She stared at me, seeming uninterested in Keon's offer. So, the act in her prison cell, was that just fake?

As much as the cold, dark evil of this ghost wanted to hurt me, I had to figure out why she wanted me... and it clearly wasn't for Keon. "It's me you're after not the stone, so tell me what you really want?"

She half laughed. "What we all do, Selena. Freedom. You want out of this prison, and I want to be free of needing a host's body. I want to move with free will, and I think you can offer me that. I sense the power in you, I feel it when I've touched you. There's something powerful inside you, and if I can just get a hold of it--"

"She wants to possess you again," Seth spoke up, his voice firm. "To drain you, just as she's doing to Nova, and will then kill you. I won't allow it."

"You won't allow it," she reiterated it, louder, then began chuckling. "Such a shame. I mean, you are a dead girl walking Selena. The bounty on your head will get you killed, and if not, I hear your vampire keeper will complete the job. So, why not let me join forces with you for a short while to ensure you get revenge against everyone who's wronged you?"

"Are you insane?" I blurted.

"I've had enough of this fucking bitch." Laz grunted as he reached her side so fast I didn't see him move until his hand snatched Nova by the throat. A savage roar tore from his chest, but in that same second, he flew across the room and slammed into the metal gates. He dropped to the ground with an aching grunt.

With a flick of her hand, all the guys suddenly flew

backward, hitting the walls and gate, their moans piercing my soul. But my gaze never left Nova. Hard and harsh, her stare grated over me.

A newfound terror came at me, savagely ripping at my insides. She grinned wickedly, and her whispers floated in the air. "You and I could be unstoppable. We could kill so many. It will be unmerciful."

"Are you mad? That will never happen," I said, my voice trembling from how furious she'd made me. "I've fought for freedom my whole life, so do you really think I'd give up so easily? Especially now that I have found four men who I love? You are crazier than I thought if you think I don't cherish my life to fight until my very last breath."

Her nose wrinkled and brow pinched as her lips peeled back in a show of anger, in a threat. "Then your last breath it will be."

Still fisting the stone, she came at me, silent words falling from my moving lips, words of magic.

The word, *run*, repeated in my mind, but there was no escape. And I had enough of running. I'd lived with hate my whole life, but it ended now.

The air hummed with magic.

My instincts kicked in, and when Nova reached me, I hurled my fist right into her face, having had enough of every damn thing. A horrible pain shot up my arm from the hit, and I shook my arm out, stepping back. "Get the hell out of my life."

She groaned, taken aback from my attack, and swayed on her feet. When she glanced up, fire burned in her eyes as blood trickled from her nose, running across her upper lip and around the edge of her mouth. "You fucking bitch."

That time, she seemed to grow in size, and fear ricocheted within me. I didn't want to be here, not in prison, and definitely not facing a crazy-ass ghost. Something rushed right past me as I was blown back when an explosion of air struck me. I fell into Keon's arms. He'd caught me and was holding me tight. But my eyes never left Nova.

Seth towered over her, his palm pressed flat against her chest. He drove her up against the wall. Her breaths rushed out of her mouth like Seth pressed the life force out of her body.

Nova writhed and thrashed, scratching at him. But it only took seconds for her to go from screaming in rage to screaming in terror. Her entire body shook... in fact, the entire room trembled. Dust cascaded from the ceiling and the gate groaned as if it were bending from the sheer energy in the air.

Keon held me tighter, but I couldn't take my gaze from Seth. His power commanded my attention as sparks of white energy rippled outward from his hand on Nova's chest.

I stiffened, staring at the agony across her face. And just as fast as it began, Seth stepped back, releasing her.

Nova collapsed to the ground in a heap. Her arm sprawled outward and her fingers unfurled. The bright green stone rolled from her palm.

I shrank in against Keon, my heart thundering in my chest.

She didn't move, didn't seem to breathe.

We all moved, staring down at her. I had no idea what to expect... my chest rose and fell hard, but Nova's never did.

"Is she..." I couldn't say the word. I never really knew Nova. It had all been a lie. The ghost had taken this woman's body and controlled her.

"She didn't survive," Seth told us, sorrow darkening his voice. "The spirit had drained her, and the girl had been too weak to fight back."

I might not have known the real Nova, but the agony of her losing her life had my chest tightening. She lost her life because of me.

"And the ghost?" I asked, my voice strangled.

Seth closed the distance between us, and he took my hands in his. There was no power in his touch, not like I'd seen him use on Nova.

"The irony is that her spell not only stopped the pain and helped to heal me, but it gave me back some of my abilities. She energized me without even knowing it. So, I sent the ghost girl into the darkest and deadliest forests in my home realm. She will never find her way out of them to ever harm anyone ever again."

I looked at Nova's body, the blood smeared across her cheek. There wasn't a flicker of life in her, even though I wished she'd awaken. It felt like hours had passed since we stepped into this room. Though it had been only minutes. I blinked back the tears for her loss.

One soul taken, another banished.

I should be happy that we found the stone. Instead, hurt and vulnerability enveloped me.

My four men surrounded me, their eyes only for me. "You are all mine," I said, desperate to feel their warmth, to stop the guilt chewing me up from the inside out.

Their eyes met mine, and they agreed. There was no

jealousy, no competition between them. The trials we'd faced brought death and terror, but it also made us one.

I fell into Seth's arms. "Please, just hold me."

And my four men did just that, and their love ignited a flicker of life and hope in my heart that maybe things might finally turn in our favor.

CHAPTER 14

SELENA

After a while, we shifted our attention to what we'd come for, the Cintamani Stone. We just stood there, staring at it. I finally reached down and picked it up and squeaked as a rush of power slid up my arm. This thing was powerful. Probably the most powerful thing I'd ever held in my life. No wonder the Warden wanted it so badly. The stone had what seemed like a glowing mist inside of it that swirled and changed from a glowing jade to a lime color and back again.

"It's Buddha's stone, so should we try to tickle its belly?" Keon asked. I was the only one who snorted. Not because it was funny, but because it was so terrible. I guess you couldn't count on a serial killer to have a sense of humor.

That thought made me laugh, though.

"Should we try it out? Make sure it's actually what we've been looking for?" Seth asked, eyeing the stone doubtfully.

"It's the right stone," answered Alaric firmly, confidence radiating in his voice.

"Fuck this. If it is the right stone, let's just use it to get out of here. Cut out the middleman," growled Laz. Of course, that sounded like a great idea, but I had a feeling that the Warden would have expected that.

"I'll try it out," Laz volunteered, grabbing the stone out of my hands. "Get the five of us out of Nightmare Penitentiary," he ordered.

Nothing happened.

"Remove Selena from the prison."

Nothing.

"Take us to the Warden."

Something was happening to Lazarus with every desperate order he gave. A grayness appeared to his skin, his eyes grew bloodshot, and his breath came out in frantic gasps.

"Stop," I cried, ripping the stone from his grip. "It's killing you."

Laz would have collapsed to the ground were it not for Keon catching him. Keon gently set him down so that he was lying on the stone floor. Laz began to shiver and moan softly to himself. "I'm so weak," he gasped.

"What just happened?" I screeched, practically throwing the stone at Alaric as I went to Laz's side. His skin was icy cold like the stone had leached something from him with every demand.

"I'm thinking the same wards that prevent prisoners from just shifting in and out of here, also contain the stone's power," said Alaric thoughtfully.

"I'm thinking that stone doesn't give away its powers for free," hissed Seth, taking a step away from it.

"I'm thinking that as well," said Keon.

"So, what do we do?" mused Alaric.

Laz gave a hacking cough that left him wheezing just then, that scared me to death.

"Maybe we just give the stone to the Warden and he'll end up getting all his power drained," I murmured as I stroked Laz's hair.

"That would only be a temporary solution," said Alaric, shaking his head. "I'm sure that Laz's strength will replenish once his healing power kicks in. And there's no guarantee that the Warden would have the same reaction. He's unlike anything I've come across. His power is immense."

Laz shot him a glare at the insinuation that the Warden was stronger than him, which made me feel better. If he was up to a dick-measuring contest, then maybe he wasn't as bad off as I'd thought.

Sure enough, in about an hour, Laz was strong enough to stand up. In that time, Keon had taken Nova's body to the doctor and called in finding her dead. Laz was still incredibly weak, but at least the guys wouldn't have to drag him all the way out of the pit. We'd spent the hour brainstorming, and we hadn't come up with much.

Except we all agreed that we couldn't trust the Warden to live up to his agreement with Alaric.

"There're no wards in the Warden's office," Keon suddenly said, making me jump as his words echoed around the stone hallway. "I bet the stone works in there."

"I can create something to mimic the stone. Hopefully, he won't be able to read the magical signature, and we can use the actual stone while he's distracted by the fake one."

"You can do that?" I asked Seth in amazement.

He smiled at me shyly. "Like I said, some of my powers seem to be coming back with the use of Nova's healing magic and the longer that I'm with you," he admitted.

"It's because she's your mate," said Alaric reluctantly. We both stared at him in amazement, but he just shrugged. "It makes sense. If the rest of us are your mates, then I doubt he's the odd man out. And everyone knows that a fae's mate increases their powers. It sure as hell is not increasing because of his daily beatings."

My face flushed, thinking about Seth being my mate. About all of them being my mates. It seemed crazy. And too good to be true, but at the same time… it just felt so right.

"Alright, do your magic, faerie boy," said Keon, breaking the moment.

Seth hissed at him, and I giggled. My laugh soon faded away as Seth picked up a small grey rock from the floor and immediately transformed it to look exactly like the Cintamani Stone that Alaric was holding.

"Incredible," said Alaric, impressed, while examining the two pieces before he eyed Seth speculatively. "Guess you are good for something."

I rolled my eyes. And Seth just snorted, obviously not offended.

"I'll make the wish to get us out of here, he'll be paying the least attention to me. I'm pretty sure he still thinks I'm devoted to the prison and just fucking Selena for fun."

Laz growled at Keon's statement, and I decided it was time to go. The boys were getting out of hand. I didn't blame them, though. Being this close to freedom was enough to make anyone edgy. Dread curled in my gut at that moment, and I tried to push it away. Everything was going to be fine. I was with four incredibly powerful supernaturals. We could stand up to the Warden.

Alaric led the way to the Warden's office. And Seth shrunk the Cintamani Stone to fit into Keon's pocket so that it would be out of sight but easily accessible for him to get us out. I just hoped that Keon was right about there being no wards in the Warden's office. I didn't know what we'd do otherwise. There was no plan B.

Laz was still incredibly weak and slowed our procession down. By the time we got to the office, there was a sheen of sweat over his face and his breath was back to being labored. Good thing we only needed Keon to ask for one wish. I didn't know that we could be down by two and pull this off.

"Come in," purred the Warden after Alaric knocked on the door.

It felt a bit like I was having a heart attack.

The five of us walked into the Warden's office. I knew the guy could smell fear; I was doing all I could not to pee myself. While the other four were pulling off calm and collected perfectly. Apparently, I needed to take acting lessons.

"Did you find it?" the Warden asked, standing from his desk; a feverish, excited glint in his eyes. I could smell his arousal in the air, not from any of us, but from the chance to have a new 'precious'.

Sorry J.R.R. Tolkien, had to go there.

"I've got it right here," said Alaric, casually pulling the fake stone from his pocket. My gaze got sidetracked on my glowing orb that was resting to the left of me on a new set of bookshelves. Like always, an intense longing hit my body, so painful it was hard to stay upright at seeing what was mine, just out of reach.

The Warden walked over, his hand outstretched, but Alaric pulled it away a second before he grabbed it.

"When I give you this, the five of us are free," he growled.

"Yes, yes," the Warden said absentmindedly, his focus solely on the stone. "You've done your job."

Alaric gave him the stone, but just as he did so, I heard a muttered curse coming from Keon, who was standing to my left.

I glanced over to him and saw that he was patting his pockets frantically. "It's gone," he mouthed.

"Looking for this?" the Warden asked with a smirk, now holding two glowing stones.

Alaric reached for the real stone, but the Warden made it disappear into the mists that were starting to surround his body.

"You thought you could actually trick me?" he asked with a cold, cruel laugh. "I would have expected better from you, Alaric."

We froze as the dark, suffocating mists began to whirl around us. The same cold, clammy feeling that I'd experienced the last time I was in this office settling across my skin.

"Wait!" Seth's voice cried out.

The mists halted.

"I have something you want more than that stone."

The mists snapped back into the Warden like a rubber band.

"And what would that be," he asked, intrigued.

Seth waved his hand, and the scepter appeared, the

scepter that he needed in order to return as ruler of Fairie, the possession that was most important to him above all others.

"Seth, no," I cried out.

He ignored me, not taking his eyes off of the Warden. "I'll give you this, in exchange for our freedom and one wish from the stone to prevent you and any others from ever coming after us."

Keon pulled me against him and pressed a hand across my lips before I could say anything else. I couldn't believe he was doing this. He was giving up everything for us. I just couldn't believe it.

The Warden held us all in suspense as we watched him with bated breath. "You have a deal," he finally said, reaching for the scepter.

Seth pulled it back, and the Warden growled, the sound terrifying enough to raise the hair on the back of my neck, "You'll make a fae's bargain first. That's the only way this happens."

I didn't fully understand the scepter's power, but watching the Warden's reaction and how he'd practically become putty in Seth's hand, it must have been significant.

A tic twitched in the Warden's cheek, but he nodded curtly and stuck out his hand. Seth gripped it tightly with the one that wasn't holding the scepter and began to mutter a collection of musical words as he waved the scepter over their clasped hands. A blue glow surrounded their grip. It brightened for a second, so much that I had to close my eyes to protect them, and then it disappeared.

Seth let go of the Warden and stared at the scepter with abject longing before he practically threw it at the

Warden. Whatever magic he'd just done must have been unbreakable because no one seemed worried the Warden would renege. The Warden immediately tossed him the stone that he'd made reappear, and the five of us huddled together, just in case we needed to be touching for the magic to work.

"My power," I whispered in despair as Keon made the wish that we would be free of the Warden and all who wished us harm forever.

The lights in the Warden's office started to flicker manically... and then everything went black.

* * *

WHEN MY EYES OPENED, we were outside the gates of Nightmare Penitentiary, I could see them in the distance. And the five of us were still standing close together.

I looked at the gates, and then I looked at my mates... and I fell apart.

"Selena," Laz groaned, taking me in his arms. Seth had a stoic look on his face.

"Tell me those are happy tears, pet," begged Alaric.

"I'm so happy to be free. And I have all of you... But he'll have my power... forever," I cried as a fresh bout of tears spilled out.

"I wasn't going to let that happen," reassured Alaric with a sudden naughty grin, and hope bloomed in my chest.

Alaric pulled a glowing orb out of his pocket; my orb, and I stared at it in shock.

"But how," I gasped, tentatively reaching out for it, unable to believe this was real.

"I'm not a master criminal in name only, my sweets. While the rest of you and the Warden were enthralled with our fae's dramatic sacrifice, I was busy grabbing things I'd had my eye on for quite a while. And of course, I wasn't going to allow us to leave without your power."

"Alaric," I whispered, but I couldn't speak through my emotions. I grabbed the orb, and my power rushed back into me. A wild wind swept through my hair and it was like a million tiny electric shocks were dancing through my body.

And when it all settled down, I finally felt whole once more. It was a strange feeling to no longer feel like a part of me had been missing from my soul.

A stretch limo pulled up beside the five of us before I could really enjoy the miracle that had just occurred. I tensed, holding my hands up to defend myself and my mates from whatever was waiting inside, but the guys didn't seem worried, they seemed relaxed.

A portly man dressed in a suit just a tad too tight for him jumped out of the driver's side and practically ran towards us.

"Alaric," he cried, and I watched in amazement as the two hugged and slapped backs.

"This is Len," Alaric said, introducing the man to us. Alaric pulled me close. "And this is my queen," he told Len proudly.

Len looked like he was about to explode with happiness.

"I'm so glad to meet you. Alaric has had much to say."

"You've told people about me?" I asked, blushing. Alaric just winked at me as Len chuckled.

"Incubi write letters too," he whispered in my ear,

biting the lobe softly and sending lust shooting through my insides, because what else would he do?

"Let's go home," Alaric announced, and Len opened the back door for us to get in.

"Show off," grumbled Keon, but he didn't look too upset about being in the lap of luxury.

"Is this a dream? I'm not going to wake up and find myself lying in a pile of shit in a prison corridor?" Laz joked. We all laughed, but I knew that was how we were all actually feeling.

Len shut the door after we'd all piled into the ridiculously fancy interior, and then he hustled to the front of the car and we began to drive away.

A small squeak drew all our attention to Keon and to the pocket of his jacket where a small white, furry head poked out. The mouse from the prison.

"You brought him with us," I stated with delight. The little guy tried to save me, so to have him out of the prison too... made me smile like crazily.

"I couldn't leave behind my little buddy. I took him into the prison, and he comes out with me."

Just as I reached over to scratch his head, he ducked back inside, hiding. I had no doubt I'd see him in our new home.

Across from me, Seth was looking pensively out the window, watching the prison fade from view. I grabbed his hand and just held it, not knowing what to say. What can you say when someone gives up their world for you?

"We'll get your kingdom back for you, brother," announced Alaric, and the guys all murmured in agreement.

Seth smiled at all of them and pulled me over so that I was cuddled against him.

We didn't say a word for the rest of the car ride. We just sat there, lost in our thoughts.

We were free.

CHAPTER 15

SELENA

*A*laric was rich. I mean I'd known he was a crime lord and controlled a bunch of stuff, but I hadn't quite comprehended what that meant.

Evidently, it meant he was lord of the universe because he had houses all over the world, a fleet of luxury cars, two private planes, and who knows what else.

I was seriously questioning his sanity. How he ever thought it was a good idea to end up in Nightmare Penitentiary when he had all of this was beyond me.

Standing in front of the contemporary modern glass mansion on two acres of private beach just south of Santa Monica, I was definitely realizing just how rich Alaric actually was.

It was overwhelming. It felt like too much coming from the horror of the prison. It was like I'd waken up in Wonderland, nothing felt real.

We were all exhausted as we walked into our new home. The adrenaline rush from getting out of prison long since faded into a bone-deep exhaustion that only months of rest and relaxation could cure. I gazed past the perfect furnishings and walked right to the back wall that was made of nothing but smooth glass and looked out upon the ocean.

The sun was fading, and an explosion of pinks and purples painted the sky. I watched it in awe, wondering if I'd ever seen anything so breathtaking.

Would I be able to keep this feeling forever? This sense of gratitude and peace, like I'd been reborn and given a new lease on life. Would it fade in time, the feeling that the world was limitless for me now?

I hoped not.

I pulled a small chunk of rock from my pocket. A piece of the wall of the prison. I'd keep it as a reminder of where I'd been, and how far I'd come.

"I thought you would like it here," said Alaric as he sidled up next to me. He pressed a button on his phone and the glass in front of me started to slide away until I could feel the ocean air on my face. The windows continued to open until the entire wall was open to the ocean. It was incredible.

"It doesn't feel real," I admitted to him as I watched the waves crash against the shore. Lake Michigan was enormous and looked like it stretched out forever in some places, but this was on a whole other level. "I keep expecting the Warden and his guards to show up at any minute and drag me away. Or even Julian, I guess."

"Nothing is ever going to hurt you again," Alaric swore fiercely.

There had been a lot of talk like that from the guys while we were in prison. And while I'd been grateful, I'd never believed them, not really.

It felt a lot easier to believe with the breeze on my face and the seagull floating over the sparkling water.

"I think I'm ready for bed," I told him, everything just crashing over me. It had been one never-ending...thing, and I felt like I could sleep for days.

"Alright, pet," Alaric murmured, kissing the top of my head. Those two words sending a little flutter to my insides. But my exhaustion quickly snuffed out anything from growing.

After I said goodnight to the others, and even though it was only seven pm, Alaric led me up one of several flights of stairs. I knew I would want to spend hours exploring the house tomorrow, but right now all I was interested in was my bed. Heck, I'd even take my prison cot set up in one of the bedrooms, as long as the cot wasn't actually in the prison. I was so tired.

That thought disappeared when Alaric opened a door and led me to an enormous bedroom, fit for a queen. The one wall faced the ocean and was made completely of glass windows, just like the wall in the living room. There was a large balcony outside that I just knew I would be spending my mornings on for as long as we were here.

There was a California King set up along the wall across from the windows, so you could just sit in bed and watch the waves if you wanted to. The decor was mini-malistic and modern, a mixture of ocean blues and sand colors making the room feel like an extension of outside. There was a chest of drawers and a sitting area with a light blue tufted couch on one of the other walls, and just beyond that was a doorway that led into a closet that could house a few cars if need be. It was overflowing with women's clothes that I knew would fit me perfectly. Alaric made sure to show me the drawers that were full of lingerie…you know, just in case.

Through another doorway, there was the bathroom of my dreams… if I'd ever spent time dreaming about what my idea of the perfect bathroom this would be it. Another glass wall lined one side of the bathroom, an enormous oval tub set in front of it, so you could bathe with a view. Across from the bathtub, there was a shower with pale aqua glass tile covering the walls, six showerheads placed throughout. You could have a party there if you wanted to.

And yes, my mind went to who I would invite to that party.

Two separate vanities were on the other walls with enough counter space to make a girl's makeup and hair dreams come true.

It was all perfect, and completely overwhelming.

"Do you like it?" Alaric asked, and I jumped because I'd kind of forgotten he was there while I was drooling over the bathroom. Alaric looked a little anxious, like my answer meant everything to him. I wasn't used to seeing him so vulnerable.

"It's all beyond amazing," I assured him. "This house is the stuff of dreams."

"It's my favorite of my homes, but I had things redone while in prison…hoping you'd like them," he admitted, nervously. And my heart threatened to beat out of my chest. "I redid this room for you. It was always meant to be yours."

I swooned and then walked over to him and gave him a soft kiss. "I couldn't have dreamed up a better place," I told him, and he puffed up his chest and smiled like I'd just complimented his cock.

"Do you want me to run you a bath?" he asked, gesturing to the heaven-like set up now at my disposal.

I was tempted for half a second until I was hit with another wave of exhaustion. The tub would have to wait. I'd gotten a quick shower while on the plane that flew us here, so at least I didn't smell like the prison anymore.

"I'll try it out in the morning," I told him, before slipping past him and back into the bedroom. I threw the sheets back and climbed in, letting out a sigh of pleasure; it was so freaking soft, like Alaric had captured a cloud and made it my bed.

"Goodnight, pet," Alaric whispered against my skin, but I was asleep before I could answer.

* * *

I woke up with a gasp, tearing myself from the clutches of a nightmare. For a second, I wasn't sure where I was. And then I remembered.

I wasn't in Nightmare Penitentiary anymore.

I was safe.

I was free.

It was dark outside. I could see stars flickering through the windows, which I hadn't seen before growing up in a big city. But we were isolated out here. No neighbors for at least a mile.

The silence was almost unnerving. I'd grown used to the never-ending moans and cries of the prisoners. They were like a morose version of white noise by the end. It was going to take a while to get used to sleeping without the screams.

I thought about trying to go back to sleep; a quick glance at the clock told me it was only two am, but I felt wired. I'd already slept for longer than I usually did in prison. I got out of bed and walked over to the windows and undid the latch so that I could slip out onto the balcony. There was a slight nip in the air, and I savored the fresh, saltiness around me. There was a dim light down below that illuminated the water's edge enough that I could see the waves slowly dancing against the sand.

I took a few deep breaths, feeling my power flickering up and down my spine. The feeling grew and grew until my body was a live wire, desperate to release energy. I suddenly roared into the heavens, my power striking out into the air as storm clouds gathered in the distance. Lightning strikes reverberated across the water and sheets of rain fell, soaking the thin nightgown that I'd changed into. I laughed as the wind sped up and whirled around me, thrashing my hair against my face.

I pushed the storm until the rain was thick like a curtain, and the previously calm waves were crashing and snarling against the rocks and shore. I relished in my power, in the ability to use it at will.

"Selena," Seth's voice floated through the darkness. I shouldn't have heard it, the thunder and lightning battering the air around me should have drowned it out, but I heard it, nevertheless. *Mate*

I looked behind me and Seth was standing there, shirtless, in a pair of black silk pants. His hair was tousled and wet from the miniature hurricane I had created.

It was the awe in his eyes that really caught my attention, though. He looked at me like I was priceless, powerful, the most beautiful thing he'd ever witnessed. Which was saying a lot since I'd now seen firsthand the beauty of Fairie.

I held out my hand to him, and he walked towards me until we were standing face to face.

"I can scarcely believe you're real sometimes," he told me, his voice breaking through the storm. A sob hitched in my throat. We hadn't talked about what he'd given up for me, not really. A million thank you's wouldn't be enough.

I didn't feel worthy.

"You gave up the scepter for me," I finally said. "Why would you do that?"

His gaze was shining with vulnerability. "Don't you know by now that I would do anything for you, Selena? I would go through every strike of those whips, give up every kingdom in every world, just so I could be with you."

"I'm not worth that," I told him honestly, my self-doubt creeping through. It would probably take a lifetime to undo what my mother and Julian had done to my inner psyche.

"You're worth everything," he swore fiercely.

Seth

THE RAIN suddenly slowed to a drizzle as soon as the words came out of my mouth. I just stared at her perfect face, knowing I'd never get tired of looking at it, never get tired of hearing her say my name or feel her touch. My heart raced with the depth of my feelings.

How did I get here so fast? Willing to give up anything and everything to keep her with me.

I guess it was true that when you found your soulmate, you just knew. Out of all the beings in the universe, there was no doubt in my mind that she was who I was meant to be with. Her blue eyes filled with wonder, as if we're sharing the same thoughts. And I just... I need her to be with me forever.

I lifted my hand and softly caressed her cheek. I felt her heartbeat quicken as we continued to gaze at each other.

"Tell me what you're thinking," I said roughly.

I'm terrified now that we're out, that she'll change her mind about me. I know it's a stupid thing to think; her love for me is so tangible I can practically taste it. So strong it could knock me over.

But still that little voice in my head tells me that I could lose her just like I have lost everyone else. And I know that, unlike the others that I've lost, there would be no coming back from losing her...

"I'm thinking that I love you, that I can't believe you're mine... I can't believe what you gave up for me," she answers in that sweet voice of hers that gives me goosebumps every time I hear it.

My arms wrapped around her shoulders, clutching her as the rain continued to fall. At this point, it almost felt like it was caressing my skin.

"Someday you'll understand just what you mean to me," I told her.

"Make love to me," she pleaded.

I tensed for a moment, wondering if she was really ready. We'd been… through a lot lately. But I didn't see any doubt in her eyes as she pleaded with me.

"Selena, we don't have to," I told her, even though my body was already ready for her. It was always ready for her.

She put her hand to my lips. "I need you. I need to feel you against me, to know that we really survived, that we're really out of that place. I want you to make love to me because I love you."

Her eyes didn't leave mine as she spoke, and I saw the mixture of desire and surrender in them. My fingers slid up her spine as I gripped her neck. Both of us moved in perfect harmony, and our mouths collided. I took control of the kiss, pouring myself into her. Each swipe of her tongue against mine was a balm to my battered soul.

Her hands moved down my shoulders, over my arms, caressing my rain-drenched skin, and then back up again. I loved the feel of her touching me. It had never been that way before. I couldn't get enough. The kiss continued as we touched each other.

It was as if I was experiencing everything for the first time.

My mouth moved against her throat, kissing her in that place right below her ear that I knew drove her wild. I moved back to her lips and took her head in my hands, making sure she was looking into my eyes, making sure that she could see how crazy I was about her. That she was everything to me.

I led her out of the rain and into the lavish suite Alaric had prepared for her. Both of us were dripping water all over the wood floor as I led her into the bathroom and then started the water. Once the steam started to build, signaling that the water was warm, we slowly undressed each other and then I led her into the shower.

I filled my hand with body wash, turned her back to my front, and began to wash her. I started at her neck, messaging and lathering the soap, moving ever so slightly down her shoulders.

"I want to spend the rest of my life worshiping you," I whisper against her ear. "I'm going to make you smile every day. You'll never know pain again." She leaned back against me as I moved to her chest.

"Seth," she whimpered as I paid special attention to the rosy tips on her perfect breasts.

Once I was done washing her, we were both desperate for more. I needed to be inside her. I needed it to feel whole. Her eyes were brimming with desire, echoing the need that was in mine. I couldn't wait any longer.

I pressed her back against the wall and found her mouth once again, pouring out every ounce of love I felt from my body. I wanted her to feel how deeply I was in love with her. She reached for my dick, trying to line it up.

"Selena," I gasped, smiling against her skin.

"Make love to me, Seth," she begged.

"I have to taste you first," I whispered, pushing the wet hair from her cheek and smiling before massaging and kneading her breasts as she writhed against me. I dropped to my knees and then lifted her legs, throwing them over my shoulders. She cried out at the first swipe of my tongue. I pressed against her clit, moving in circles, then up and down. Her body stiffened, and I knew she was about to climax.

"Holy crap," she panted as I slipped my finger inside her wet heat and sucked her even harder. Another finger joined the first, and I pushed deeper, crooking them at just the right angle I knew would drive her mad. She burst apart on my tongue and fingers. And it was one of the most glorious things I'd ever seen. Our breathing was erratic, and I swore my heart was thumping loud enough to reverberate around the room.

I set her down as gently as I could, considering how desperate I was to get inside of her. Without warning, I stood and slammed into her. Her eyes squeezed tight as she struggled to accommodate me.

"You okay, sweetheart?" I asked.

She nodded quickly, and I kissed her as I rocked slowly in and out of her. This was heaven. I wanted to live in this sweet pussy.

"Seth," she whimpered. "It's too much."

Everything about her was incredible. We moved against each other, completely lost in what was happening. I began to move faster as my orgasm built.

"I'm going to cum," she moaned.

"Yes. Love the way you grip my cock, sweet girl," I said through gritted teeth. My fingers digging into the flesh of her hips, pulling her against me harder as I thrusted to meet her.

This was it, I was ruined.

"Selena!" I cried out as my climax hit me hard. Her answering cry was music to my ears as she followed me over the edge.

"I love you," I whispered against her lips as I turned the water off. I grabbed a towel, and carried her out of the bathroom.

I wasn't even close to being finished with her.

We had a lot to celebrate.

Selena

WE STAYED at Alaric's house by the ocean for a month, just healing. Physically we were all alright, but mentally and emotionally… that was a whole other story. Alaric was the steadiest of all of us, being that he'd walked into the prison voluntarily to find out its secrets and find trinkets to help secure his territory. Evidently, along with my orb, he'd grabbed a treasure trove of other things.

It was a good thing that the Warden couldn't come after us or send anyone else after us.

I'm sure he was missing all of his 'pretties' really badly. That made me smile.

Our month was spent walking along the beach, cook-outs on the deck, watching the sunset…and lots and lots of sex.

Honestly, it was a miracle that my vagina was still functioning at this point. Having an incubus around to make sure that everyone was able to perform constantly… was a bonus.

Thank goodness for supernatural healing.

We were packing to head down south to check in on Alaric's territories and holdings. Alaric had already been away from the business long enough. He'd promised we'd come back to this place often, but as I stared out at the waves one last time, I was already missing it.

The weather was echoing my emotions, no doubt

influenced by my power. The sky was dark and stormy and there was a perpetual cool mist in the air. The sea was a stormy gray color, and the waves thrashed against the sand.

"Selena, time to go," called Laz, and I wistfully walked away from my view of the ocean.

Laz wrapped an arm around my waist and kissed the top of my head. He didn't say anything to reassure me, and I loved that about him. Sometimes I just needed to be alone with my thoughts. For a hellhound, he was very cool-headed.

We loaded into a black Escalade that had so many gadgets that I was afraid to touch anything, and it took us to a nearby private airport where one of Alaric's planes was waiting. As soon as we got into the luxurious all-black space that was the epitome of sexy, fitting since its owner was an incubus, Keon and Laz settled down to play some video games while I snuggled with Seth on one of the four couches. Alaric was in the back already taking calls. With how busy he'd been since we'd gotten out, I didn't know how he'd survived not being able to communicate twenty-four seven with his people.

"Doing okay, sweetheart?" Seth asked.

"I hope there's water where we're going. I think it helps my power," I admitted with a shrug. "That place was the closest thing to a home I've ever experienced. I'm just sad we had to leave."

"Knowing how crazy Alaric is about you, I'm sure that this next place is going to be just as good," he reassured me.

That mollified me a bit and I snuggled closer to him, deciding to take a nap since I'd learned that planes were not my favorite things on the flight out here. What exactly did people enjoy about being trapped in a tin can in the sky? Even the most lavish tin can scared me, I'd decided.

Four hours later, and the plane was touching down. I looked outside at the tall pine trees surrounding the airstrip. It wasn't the ocean, but it was still beautiful.

Once the plane landed, Alaric took my hand and led me towards the front of the plane. When the door opened, I was hit by a wave of muggy air. It was freaking hot here.

I was so distracted by the heat and the new surroundings that I almost missed the small crowd of people gathered to the left of us. As soon as they saw us a loud cheer rang out. A broad, beautiful grin burst over Alaric's face at the sight of some of his people and I swear the crowd swooned.

Keeping me close, he led us down the stairs and towards the crowd. They were immediately trying to shake his hand and hug him, but their endeavors were sidelined a bit by the fact that Alaric hadn't let go of me. The crowd quieted when they noticed my three other lovers following behind us.

"It's good to be home," Alaric said simply. Evidently, that was enough because the crowd cheered again and then everyone loaded into the many vehicles on the tarmac, leaving another large Escalade for our group to get in.

There were two huge beast-like men in the driver and front passenger seat. Alaric introduced them as his bodyguards. Keon snorted at the idea. And I kind of followed along, because he didn't really need bodyguards. Alaric growled at Keon before giving me a wink as he tucked me closer to his side, and I just shook my head.

We had only driven for about ten minutes when I plastered my face to the window. There was water, lots of it. There were rivers and streams. Deer kept popping in and out of the thick forest. Birds were fluttering from tree to tree. It was like we'd stepped into a forest from a storybook.

"What do you think, pet?" Alaric asked.

"It's gorgeous," I admitted in awe. "It's so different from the beach house. But just as beautiful."

"I knew you'd like it," Alaric responded cockily.

The SUV turned the corner and I sat up in my seat nervously. There was a stone wall at least twelve feet tall in front of us, and beyond that…a freaking castle.

"Showoff," Laz muttered as gates embedded within the stone wall slowly opened and we pulled onto a smooth paved road that appeared to lead straight towards the castle.

There were buildings everywhere. Men, women, and children were six deep on the sidewalks waving excitedly as our vehicle passed. There was an entire city here, and from what Alaric had told me, a whole country beyond that.

Alaric rolled the windows down and waved back at his people.

A few women appeared to pass out when they saw him, like he was some kind of rock star. I just rolled my eyes and gave Alaric a side eye.

The rest of the guys were staring out of their window.

"Tell me we're going to be staying in that castle," Keon said excitedly.

Alaric gave him a look like, *what do you think?*

"No killing inside the walls," Alaric warned him with a growl.

Keon held up his hands. "Wouldn't dream of it."

We pulled up to the front of the castle and I got out, a little dazed as I stared up at it. It was the same dark stone as the wall surrounding the city. There were at least twelve turrets that I could see with enormous windows and balconies peppered all over it.

"Welcome home, Selena," Alaric purred before he suddenly pulled me into a kiss that had me forgetting everything but the way that he set my soul on fire.

He pulled away from me and then took my hand and led us around the vehicles. The castle was set on a hill so the city was spread out before it. While we'd been driving, Alaric's people had gathered on the road surrounding the castle, their cheers growing louder and louder.

"I've missed you all," Alaric told the crowd, his voice somehow amplified. "My mission was a success. And we will never fear our enemies again."

With that announcement the crowd's cheers grew into a roar and I smiled thinking about the protective talisman and the host of other things Alaric had managed to poach from the Warden. That didn't even include the things he'd been sending his people throughout his stay in Nightmare as he discovered them.

Alaric held up his hands to quiet the crowd. "But I've brought you something else," he announced proudly, pulling me close to his side.

"I have brought you back a queen."

The crowd's roars grew so loud that it was deafening.

Laz, Keon, and Seth came up behind us as Alaric held

our hands up in the air. He then grabbed me and dipped me in a kiss like I'd only seen in the movies.

Of course, his people loved that. I was going to need new eardrums after all of this.

Their enthusiasm was encouraging, though.

"Welcome home, my queen," Alaric purred after our kiss had ended.

I grinned up at him before my gaze flicked to my other mates.

I'd been a slave, and then a prisoner before I'd met these men. I'd never dreamed of being a queen.

Maybe happily ever afters could exist after all.

I really liked the sound of that.

EPILOGUE

SELENA

3 Years Later

Being patient was a bitch. Even with the new life we'd built for ourselves, Julian still lurked in the back of my mind, a sore that was still festering and wouldn't heal until he was gone. We had a life to create, so there wasn't time to figure out a plan to get past the army that Julian had surrounded himself with. I'd had to ignore it because a world in which Julian still existed was a world I had trouble sleeping in. Despite how powerful I'd grown, and how powerful all my mates were… Julian was the bogeyman under the bed, waiting to pounce. The only creature who could destroy the slice of heaven we'd built for ourselves.

But that all ended tonight.

Alaric's spies had been watching the vampires had informed us that Julian had recently eased up. Our disappearance giving him a false sense of security that we were no longer a threat. Or perhaps something else was making him feel safer these days. I liked to think he feared retribution from my men and me.

Julian was at his decadent mansion, right on the lake's edge tonight, waiting for the call-girl he'd ordered. Evidently, he'd outgrown the sirens he used to favor and was looking for something a bit more... exotic.

It had been way too easy to make sure that the call-girl never arrived. And with some of Seth's fae power put into an amulet I wore around my neck, I'd been transformed into an enticing creature that he'd never suspect was me. I got out my compact mirror and checked my appearance one more time, making sure I hadn't suddenly changed back somehow. Long blonde hair cascaded over my shoulders down my back and sparkling brown eyes stared back at me from a stranger's flawless face. Perfect. I looked almost angelic like this. It was fitting.

The guys had wanted to kill Julian for me. But I'd refused.

Some things were just too personal to allow someone else to handle .

Killing Julian was one of those things.

Of course, the guys were nearby, just in case things went south. But I knew I wouldn't need them. When you wanted something this bad, there was no other option but success.

The car that Julian had ordered for his escort pulled up to the gates outside of Julian's estate. There was a formidable stone wall that surrounded the property, covered top to bottom in enchantments. The only way you were getting in was if he invited you.

Theoretically.

I was pretty confident that my powers would have

allowed me to get through if need be, but this way was easier.

Julian answered the gate's call himself, solidifying that he was alone, or relatively alone. If his servants had been around, there was no way that he would have opened the gate himself. That escort we'd bribed to stay away tonight really should have paid me for saving her from this call. Because whatever Julian had planned for her, he hadn't wanted any witnesses.

I took several deep breaths as the car wound its way down the road that led to the monstrosity of a mansion Julian call home and that I'd been to many times for parties and events while growing up. It probably would have seemed gorgeous to a normal person, but I knew too well the atrocities that occurred here, and it would forever seem like a nightmarish place to me.

We pulled up to the front door, and I thanked the driver and gathered my purse. I was shaking a bit, not from fear, but from the adrenaline that was coursing through my veins in anticipation of what was to come. I could feel four sets of eyes on my back and my body flushed, knowing who was watching me from somewhere in the shadows.

Like I said, the enchantments were 'theoretically' impossible to get past.

I nodded to a single guard who had been stationed outside the front entrance, and he opened the door to let me in. Once inside, I pulled out the accessories that Julian had requested from the escort service.

A pair of cat ears.

Things were about to get weird.

The guard shut the door behind me, leaving me alone in the giant entryway that could easily fit a small house.

Sinuous footsteps at the top of the grand staircase straight ahead alerted me of Julian's presence. He stood there, dressed in a pair of black lounge pants and a crimson silk robe, of all things, loosely belted so that his smooth chest was proudly on display.

Ick factor times one hundred.

"Hello, pussycat," he purred as he descended the stairs. I wasn't exactly sure what I was supposed to do at this point. His instructions he'd given the agency hadn't been exactly clear. I wasn't psyched about potentially having to crawl around the ground and start meowing, but I'd do it if I had to as long as the night ended with his death.

Julian's footsteps were torturously slow. For a vampire who could move from zero to sixty in a second without a thought, this was ridiculous. He was really going for the drama tonight.

Finally, he stood in front of me.

"Meow," I squeaked, and a predator's grin stretched out across his face, his incisor teeth lengthening and sharpening as his arousal grew.

So gross.

He held up a collar attached to a leash, and I smiled demurely as he placed it around my neck and walked me across the room to one of the three hallways that led into the rest of the house. Luckily, he was allowing me to walk as a two-legged creature, and not a four-legged one.

Looking surreptitiously around, I noticed that there weren't any guards standing anywhere. I'd still only seen the one out front. He'd really been getting confident, hadn't he?

What was that phrase? "Pride cometh before the fall," or something like that? Whatever it was, it fit this situation perfectly.

Julian led me towards a sumptuous velvet couch in his entertainment room. There was an assortment of sex toys laid out on an enormous ottoman, along with a bowl of white liquid that I suspected was milk. Or at least hoped was milk.

There was also a whip. But we were going to be very much done before he ever got the chance to use that.

"Sit down, little kitten," Julian ordered. I obediently sat down, my heartbeat feeling like it was about to beat out of my chest. Luckily for me, my racing heart could easily be mistaken for fear, and since this was a situation where anyone would feel that, Julian was eating it up.

"I have so many plans for you, little kitten," he murmured, his pupils blowing up with his arousal until you could only see a slivered ring of white. "But maybe I'll just get a little taste before we start the fun."

Like the true asshole he was, he didn't wait for my agreement before he pounced, his teeth slicing into my flesh, with no concern for my pain. A vampire could make a bite feel beyond good if it wanted. Julian obviously did not want to. Dick!

I had once been terrified of this exact scenario, but I knew there was a wide grin stretched across my face right now. I welcomed the gulps of blood he was taking, knowing they were bringing him that much closer to his destruction.

It took seconds for the sedative to take effect . I'd injected myself with a serum made from a plant that was harmless to sirens, but knocked a vampire on the ass.

He'd feel everything though, even as he laid there, unable to move.

"What?" he croaked as I unlatched him from my throat and laid him down on the couch. His fingers twitched for a moment as he struggled to move. And then he was perfectly still.

Grinning at him, I slowly and dramatically removed the necklace from my neck and watched as the panic and terror built in his eyes as my features transformed and I once again looked like my true self.

A wheezing sound came out of his mouth as he tried to say my name, and I cackled in delight.

"How does it feel to be utterly powerless, Julian?" I cooed as I lifted the bottom of my dress and pulled the stake from the holster around my thigh.

Silly, stupid, conceited vampire... didn't even bother to check if I'd had a weapon. You live, you learn... ha! Not in this case.

Bloody droplets of sweat beaded down his face as I stroked the oak stake reverently. A wet patch appeared at his crotch, the sharp scent of his urine filling the air.

"I want you to know that after tonight, I'll never think about you again." I paused, because duh, theatrical effect. I'd had a lot of time to plan for this moment. And it was going perfectly, well, besides the fact that I was wearing a pair of cat ears.

"But I'm sure you'll think about me every moment... when you're in hell," I finally finished.

With that dramatic pronouncement, I lifted the stake and stabbed the bastard right in his fucking heart. And I laughed with psychotic glee as his ashes completely covered my body; he'd literally exploded.

I sat there for a moment, just soaking in the fact that he was really and truly gone. That this once insignificant slave of the vampires had brought his demise.

I felt... free.

I stood up and shook myself off, getting at least most of the ash off while I ripped off the cat ears and threw them on the pile of what was left of Julian.

On my way out, I made a side trip to the kitchen, where I turned on all the burners on the multiple gas stovetops. I then placed the bomb Alaric had created for me on the marble countertop and set the timer so that it would go off in an hour, long enough for the gas to permeate the immediate area. When this was all done, there would be nothing left and Julian would just be a bad memory, a memory soon forgotten and replaced.

The sky was softening as I walked out the front door of the mansion, the guard nowhere to be seen. It would be sunrise soon, but everything already looked brighter to me as I strode down the road.

"You can come out now," I called out, a giggle erupting from my chest from the euphoria and adrenaline rush I was experiencing.

Almost as one, they all stepped from the shadows of the trees that lined the inside of the fence. I ran towards Alaric and jumped into his arms, not worrying for a second that he wouldn't catch me. Because he would always catch me. I could always count on him. I could always count on all of them.

"Is it done, little siren?" Laz asked, coming up behind me so that I was sandwiched between him and Alaric.

"Yes, and it was perfect," I announced proudly.

"I know, I've got it on video," announced Keon gleefully, staring at a video playing on a phone in his hands.

"Why didn't you tell us we could watch?" hissed Seth, punching Keon in the shoulder.

Keon ignored him and gave a loud whoop as the sound of me staking Julian played from his phone.

"Those kitten ears were cute, darlin'," Keon growled with a wink and of course I blushed because Keon still had that effect on me even after all these years of being with him twenty-four seven.

"Want to stay for the fireworks?" Seth asked, pulling me away from Alaric and Laz.

"Definitely," I nodded.

"How about watching the show on the lake?" asked Alaric with a grin, and I laughed in delight.

I was different now, obviously different. There was a darkness inside of me that would never fade.

But that was alright. My men were just as dark, well, if I was being honest, much darker. So, my darkness fit me just fine.

Alaric had somehow arranged for a large speedboat to be waiting at the dock, and we all hopped in and then headed out towards the center of the lake.

We all watched the video a few more times while we waited, and then it was time.

The five of us counted down the last ten seconds like it was New Year's Eve, and then the air was filled with the sound of the explosion and our cheers as a giant fireball lit up the sky; Julian's house destroyed.

It was over, really over.

The sun was peeking over the horizon as the boat sped towards the other side of the lake where the next chapter of our life would begin. There was still so much to do, a kingdom to get back for Seth, and revenge for Laz against his so-called friend who had betrayed him. But here in this moment... I didn't have any worries about what the future would bring.

The five of us could do anything together. I was sure of that.

"Happy Birthday, little siren," Laz growled as we watched the flames of my past get smaller and smaller as the boat raced away. I grinned at him. Best. Birthday. Ever.

How things had changed.

So long ago, I thought that my birthday was the end of my life. But I'm glad to say that it was actually just the beginning of my story.

I was taught my whole life about the importance of true mates, how when you find that one wolf for you, everything falls into place.

Everyone who taught me that was a liar.

When I found my true mate, happily ever after sure as hell didn't start, but hell definitely began.

I ran away, and now I've been searching for peace for weeks as I drive around the country.

I didn't mean to take the wrong road.

I didn't mean to make it to that small town.

And I didn't mean to meet two men, who set me and my wolf on fire.

But here I am somehow, and peace is the last thing I've found.

And don't forget about the serial killer…

START READING WILD MOON TODAY

ACKNOWLEDGMENTS

Writing the last book in the Thief of Hearts was a lot of fun, but also heartbreaking as it's never easy to say farewell to characters who've lived in our hearts all this time. But this is just the beginning for Selena and her four sizzling hot men. And you never know... you might see more stories in this world coming your way. Be prepared to be blown away... Thank you for joining us on this journey.

Love

Mila & C.R. Jane

C.R. JANE

A Texas girl living in Utah now, I'm a wife, mother, lawyer, and now author. My stories have been floating around in my head for years, and it has been a relief to finally get them down on paper. I'm a huge Dallas Cowboys fan and I primarily listen to Beyonce and Taylor Swift...don't lie and say you don't too.

My love of reading started probably when I was three and with a faster than normal ability to read, I've devoured hundreds of thousands of books in my life. It only made sense that I would start to create my own worlds since I was always getting lost in others'.

I like heroines who have to grow in order to become badasses, happy endings, and swoon-worthy, devoted, (and hot) male characters. If this sounds like you, I'm pretty sure we'll be friends.

I'm so glad to have you on my team...check out the links below for ways to hang out with me and more of my books you can read!

**Join my Facebook readers' group:
www.facebook.com/groups/C.R.FatedRealm/**

Visit my website: www.crjanebooks.com/

MILA YOUNG

**Find all Mila young books at
www.milayoungbooks.com**

Best-selling author, Mila Young tackles everything with the zeal and bravado of the fairytale heroes she grew up reading about. She slays monsters, real and imaginary, like there's no tomorrow. By day she rocks a keyboard as a marketing extraordinaire. At night she battles with her mighty pen-sword, creating fairytale retellings, and sexy ever after tales. In her spare time, she loves pretending she's a mighty warrior, walks on the beach with her dogs, cuddling up with her cats, and devouring every fantasy tale she can get her pinkies on.

Ready to read more and more from Mila Young?
www.subscribepage.com/milayoung

Join Mila's **Wicked Readers group** for exclusive content, latest news, and giveaway.
www.facebook.com/groups/milayoungwickedreaders

For more information...
mila@milayoungbooks.com